Belonging After All

ALSO BY BARBARA E. SAEFKE

REMEMBER THE WORDS

Belonging After All

Barbara E. Saefke

Order this book online at www.trafford.com
or email orders@trafford.com

Most Trafford titles are also available at major online book retailers.

Cover designer and photographer: Benjamin Saefke

Printed in the United States of America.

ISBN: 978-1-4251-9105-4 (sc)
ISBN: 978-1-4251-9107-8 (e)

Trafford rev. 03/21/2011

 www.trafford.com

North America & International
toll-free: 1 888 232 4444 (USA & Canada)
phone: 250 383 6864 ♦ fax: 812 355 4082

In memory of my best friend
Donna Palm Peterson

For my Mom, Angeline Westman
The best PR person I know

In memory of my step-dad
Harry Westman

Acknowledgments

Thank you to the members of the Coffee House Writer's Guild for reading and rereading my manuscript. In special memory of Sharon Wikstrom, playwright and friend.

My family: for their unending support

Ben Saefke: who took time out of his busy photography business to design the cover and author photo

Jean Conklin: for keeping me on track to finish my second book

A big thank you to the people who helped with the final edit: Joyce Sexton, Jean Conklin, Shirley Sinderson, Joyce Fuhrman, John Hachey, Jim Saefke, Mary Anne Casey.

Thank you to Christina Normile, for being on the cover of my book. What an honor for me!

Contact Information
www.rememberthewords.com
barb@rememberthewords.com

Chapter One

He came to the same place every day for three months. The Ponte Vecchio Bridge, over the Arno River in Florence—one of Italy's most famous bridges—was where he had seen her last. She had been speaking English to one of the many jewelry shop owners and had tried on diamond rings, but hadn't bought any. She had looked at the diamonds, but was not wearing one.

She was tall and thin, like him; she wore dark green leather boots, boots that were bought for comfort and not fashion, and a long skirt that matched the green in her boots. She looked elegant in her feminine white lace blouse, with her dark curly hair flowing down her back. The beret she wore looked as if it had been made specifically for her.

If only she would come back, he would go to her and invite her for coffee. He walked slowly back and forth across the bridge, and when he finally decided to head for home he walked quickly to Via Laura, the street where he lived.

Before he made it home, he decided to stop for an espresso. While he was in line, he wondered why so many people visited Florence. It was difficult for the citizens to wander around the city, it was so crowded at times.

But then he thought of the beautiful signorina from America that he did want to return to Florence.

Someone stepped on his foot and interrupted his thoughts. He looked down and saw the green boots, then looked up quickly—and there she was. "Scusi, scusi," she said in a frantic voice.

His smile was so warm that she smiled back at him. "Get in line, Signorina. That way you stay off my feet."

She got in front of him and he was still smiling as he said, "You've been to Florence before. I see you on bridge looking at diamonds." She turned and looked at him and he took her hand. "But you wear no diamonds."

She was disturbed that he remembered seeing her before and was a bit uncomfortable that he had. "I like to look, not buy," she said, then turned back to face the front of the line.

"Are you here on business?"

Realizing he was going to keep asking questions, she turned around again. "Yes, I come almost once a month."

"How long will you be staying this time?" he asked, hoping she had several days.

"Two more days, then I travel on the third day." Why is he talking to me, she wondered. Her body felt uneasy. Logic told her to get her coffee and walk back to the hotel; but she'd been without male companionship for six years. Her heart told her to stay.

They ordered their espresso. "Come, sit outside with me." He pleaded, not really asking her.

"Outside would be nice. It's a beautiful evening."

She was drawn to his calm manner. He was older, she thought, or maybe appeared older because of his long graying hair that was swept away from his face.

"Are you busy the two days before going home?"

"I have some business tomorrow and then I have the following day free."

"Spend the day with me!" She noticed that the pleading had returned to his voice and her body felt the unease again. What she said next surprised her.

"I can meet you back here, but first I need to know your name."

"It's Rudolfo Vittori, and yours?"

"Francesca Jones."

The way she said her name excited him. He wouldn't let her go this time without finding out where to contact her. He waited until his body returned to normal before he asked, "Where are you staying?"

"At the hotel, Morandi Alla, on Via Laura 50." The excitement returned and surged through him. "Do you know where it is?" she asked. "Yes," he whispered. He looked into her blue eyes and felt more alive than he had in ages.

"You're staring at me. Why?"

"Your beauty astonishes me," answered Rudolfo, still not able to answer above a whisper.

The scent of coffee drifted from the café to the outside tables, and it reminded her of home. Why had she agreed to have coffee with him? He was a stranger in a foreign country. She had been planning to go back to America tomorrow when a business meeting came up and she had had to change her flight home. Was it fate that they had met?

He looked weary, as if he had been out walking all day. She knew from experience what that was like. She tended to walk too much herself whenever she came to Florence.

"Francesca, I come to your hotel day after tomorrow. Come downstairs at eight."

The pleading was gone from his voice and had been replaced with assurance. She couldn't think of a reason why she had agreed to have coffee with him, and now she couldn't think of a reason not to meet him. But she had a day to think about it. Tomorrow she'd ask her colleagues what they thought of the idea of meeting with Rudolfo.

"I'll be waiting on the street by the hotel, but I want to let you know that all this seems so strange to me. If I'm not there, I had second thoughts."

Dismissing that, he said, "It's dark, I walk you to hotel."

"No, Rudolfo, you don't have to walk me back." In the morning it would be light out, now it was dark. Would he pull her into an alley and she'd never see her daughter again? For some reason her body no longer felt the unease it had when they'd first met. But she was still apprehensive.

"Signorina, I want to walk you back." Oh, how badly he wanted to walk her back. They got up from their chairs, and Rudolfo said, "It is dark, I walk you back."

They walked in silence. Motor scooters drove by, couples walked hand-in-hand, and even though the air was brisk, Francesca felt a warmth she didn't understand. They turned on Via Laura to the hotel.

"I see you in two days, Francesca."

"I'll be down at eight."

He walked to his apartment, two doors down, and as he unlocked the door he thanked the gods for finding Francesca for him.

*   *   *

Rudolfo awoke early after a night of fitful sleep. Was she being nice and just saying she would meet him? Would she truly have second thoughts and have left a message for him at the hotel desk when he came to call? Several times he had gotten up and paced around his small apartment until he'd become exhausted and had returned to bed.

Last night he had called his friend, Filipo, and arranged to meet for breakfast in the morning, not telling Filipo of his good news. They were to meet outside the Duomo. As he was getting dressed, the beauty of Francesca overwhelmed his mind and body. His legs were weak and he sat down in the recliner. He glanced at his watch and knew he had to leave now so he wouldn't be late. He willed himself to stand and then the real challenge came—to walk down the fifteen steps to the street.

*   *   *

"Rudy, are you still looking for your mysterious signorina?"

"No."

"Is that all you say? What happened?"

"She step on my foot."

Filipo burst into laughter and slapped his old friend on the back. "You been looking every day and she come and step on your foot."

Rudolfo noticed what delight Filipo was getting from his story. "She stepped on my foot and I drank coffee with her."

"You see her again, yes?"

"Tomorrow. I call for her at the hotel, the Morandi Alla."

Filipo laughed again. "You have such good fortune. You just two doors down from her."

"We'll see what good fortune I have, if she'll meet me tomorrow."

"She had coffee with you, she will meet you tomorrow."

He doubted she would meet him, after all the bad luck he had had in love. It saddened Rudolfo to think of the woman who had promised to marry him, then didn't show up the day of the wedding. She had left for America to marry someone else. When he found another, she wanted him to stop being an artist and writer to earn more money so she could live comfortably. When he didn't give up his work, she left him.

Filipo had known Rudolfo for twenty years, and he knew what his friend was feeling. A life of rejection in love hopefully would make Rudolfo cautious when he met someone new.

He had been concerned when Rudolfo had mentioned his mystery signorina and had gone and looked for her to return to Florence. At last he had found her, and now Filipo worried that he would love and lose again.

"Is she as beautiful on the inside as she is on the outside?"

"Yes, Filipo," said Rudolfo with a catch in his voice.

"You love her?"

"From the moment I saw her, which scared me because of my failure at love."

"No, Rudolfo, you not failure at love. Those other women not know how to love."

Rudolfo finished his coffee and pastry. "I must go now, Filipo."

"Go where? Back to apartment to worry if she meet you or not? Come, walk with me. We walk through city."

Rudolfo knew his friend was right, he would worry all day. So they walked most of the day, stopped for dinner, and when Rudolfo arrived home he made some tea and went to bed.

*   *   *

Rudolfo rose early and read the paper. He remained hopeful that Francesca would meet him. Since it was raining so hard, he didn't know what they would do today.

Filipo had warned him on their walk not to expect too much and not to move too fast, it might scare her away. He would take his good friend's advice. They would take a walk, stop and eat, and he would have her back by nightfall. But now, with the rain, not even his heavy-duty umbrella would keep such a lovely lady dry.

*   *   *

At seven fifty-five, Rudolfo was waiting in the lobby and not in the street. At eight, Francesca started down the stairs. She looked stunning in her long black skirt with a slit up the side and a green silk blouse. He looked down and saw those green boots, boots he was beginning to associate with the beautiful signorina. "Francesca," he whispered and held out his hand, and she took it.

"I've been thinking, Rudolfo, I shouldn't be meeting with you. I don't know you. You could want to harm me."

A saddened look captured his face and he was devastated that she thought that way. Francesca saw the disheartened look in his eyes and wished she had never said it.

"No, no, Francesca, I never hurt you," said Rudolfo, trying to control the quiver in his voice, and at that moment Francesca knew he never would.

Changing the subject, she said, "What do you have planned on this rainy October day?"

"It's coming down hard. We will get wet even with umbrella."

"Why don't you come up to the hotel dining room and we can sit and have breakfast?"

"You come to my home and I make you breakfast, Francesca." He saw the hesitation in her body and didn't want her to say no. "Then you come to my home and you make us breakfast, no?" Rudolfo's face warmed with a smile.

Francesca smiled and Rudolfo went weak. "I'll come if you have coffee that you can put in a big cup and not the miniature ones they have in the cafés," she said.

"Yes, I make you big cup of coffee. I even add chocolate for you, if you like."

"I like."

He gave her his umbrella, took her hand, and led her down the two doorways to his apartment, unlocked it, then they went in. Francesca was surprised he lived so close to the hotel.

"Why is there a plaque with Bruno Cicognani's profile outside your apartment building?"

"He was a short story writer and wrote about Via Laura in one of his novels." He closed the umbrella and shook it out. "He wrote La Velia in 1921, said to be the best Italian novel of the postwar decade. He is greatly esteemed in Italian literary circles."

"That's fascinating."

They walked up the long enclosed stairway. Rudolfo, leading the way, unlocked another door at the top of the stairs. An oversized recliner looked inviting, and Francesca sat down.

"Good, you sit, I make coffee."

Francesca noticed family pictures placed around the room. One was a picture of two small children with their parents. She got out of the recliner and took a picture of a small boy and girl off the mantle. The boy had features similar to Rudolfo. Thin face, dark features, and those mesmerizing eyes. There was another picture of six children on a long couch, and the parents were standing behind them.

She started thinking of her own family. Why am I here? she asked herself silently. He has a charm and urgency about him, and the way his brown eyes look at me . . .

"Are you still wondering about the stranger you met?" asked Rudolfo when he entered the room.

How did he know what I was thinking? She felt heat rising in her neck.

"Your coffee, Francesca. In big cup with chocolate, and cream on top."

The cup looked like one her grandmother had in her china cabinet, with the matching saucer and handle that you couldn't get your finger through.

She smiled, "Thank you, Rudolfo."

"Taste it."

His eyes were now like those of the small child in the picture, all lit up with anticipation. She put the cup to her lips and tasted the coffee. "It's wonderful. Do you have more?"

"Cup not big enough for Americans. My sister like her coffee in big cup, too."

"Is your sister in America?"

"Yes, she want me to move and live with her."

"Where does she live?"

"New York."

"Would you live with your sister?"

"I been there and city too big for me."

"How many times have you been there?"

"I see all my nieces and nephews, except her youngest child." He pointed to their picture on the mantle, "I go there on their fifth birthday."

"Why their fifth birthday?"

"I go see them when they turn five, because then they old enough to remember me. I didn't think she have so many."

Francesca laughed. "Do you like America?"

"I like America. My sister drive me to New York City. City too big. I like the suburb where she live much better."

"Show me where the coffee is."

"Come this way."

She followed him down a narrow hallway and noticed a small bedroom off to the right with one dresser and an unmade bed. They got to the kitchen and he poured her more coffee and pointed to the chocolate and cream. "I don't make my bed because I just mess it up at night."

"How do you always know what I'm thinking?"

"I just know."

She decided not to let it bother her. "As much as my mother stressed the importance of making my bed, I don't either."

He could smell her musk cologne as she stood close to him. Pleasant, he thought. She continued to talk about her mother, but Rudolfo could only think of her closeness, her elbow touching his arm as she was stirring her coffee.

"Francesca," he whispered.

She stopped stirring, and without looking at him, said, "You always whisper my name."

He recovered quickly and said, "You have a name that should only be whispered."

"Tell my mother that when she gets angry at me." She put down the spoon. "I bet she would like to meet you. I mean . . . I don't know what I mean."

She turned and faced him. He was so close to her. Those eyes were waiting, waiting for what, she didn't know, and she got lost looking into those desperate brown eyes, and knew why she was in his apartment. The need she saw in him was the need she felt in her own life. Was he here to fill that void?

"Rudolfo," she whispered.

"Ah, Signorina, now you whisper my name."

"I need to sit," she said, but she couldn't manage to move past him.

"You sit, bring your coffee to front room and I make breakfast." He made himself busy and tried not to notice that she still wasn't moving away from the counter. She watched him, holding her cup to her lips.

"You go sit, Francesca, or you help." He held out a potato to her. She put down her cup and took it. "The knife is there. We will fry them. You cut into pan on stove."

The kitchen was small, the walls were a faded yellow, and the cupboards, when she saw Rudolfo open them, were mostly bare and lined with white shelf paper. When he reached for a frying pan in the top cupboard, she noticed his muscled body and the fact that he barely had to extend himself to reach it.

The wooden table off to the side was big enough for two people, with three matching chairs. One chair that must have been the one Rudolfo sat on was worn on the seat and on the wooden bars on the back.

She turned on the burner, took the knife, and started cutting the potato without saying a word, then watched the potatoes as they hit the grease and made a sizzling noise. He was next to her. This wasn't happening, she thought. It can't be. She shook her head to clear it. Maybe she would find herself back at the hotel, dreaming.

When the food was done, Rudolfo said, "We eat now, then you ask me questions."

He dished up the potatoes and eggs, and Francesca poured more coffee for herself and Rudolfo. They sat and started eating.

"You've seen me before. On the bridge?"

"Si."

"Why did you ask me to join you for coffee, after I stepped on your foot?"

"When I saw you on the bridge I want to see you again. You not come back until now."

She remembered she hadn't been able to come back. Her daughter had been sick with the measles and then she herself had caught a cold and wasn't able to travel. "Why did you want to see me again?"

"It hard to explain, even for me. At first I just want to paint you and when I thought about you, it went beyond my need to paint you. I thought of you all the time, and then you come."

"Rudolfo, your story makes me warm inside, but scares me, too. What now? I go home tomorrow."

There couldn't be more, she was leaving, and yet she felt she would be leaving something behind. Something that would make her keep coming back to Florence, even if she were sick.

"You come back," said Rudolfo, with confidence. "My nephew turns five in December. I come to America. I see you then. Where in America do you live?"

"Minnesota."

"I hear you get much snow. I come see you in December, and bring warm clothes." He made a shivering gesture. "It gets cold in Minnesota, no?"

"Yes, very cold. When you come, you can meet my daughter."

His shoulders slumped and his face paled. "Francesca married." He said it as a statement of fact, and not a question. He felt the pain in his heart and his brown eyes lost all hope.

She could tell she had hurt him. "No, Rudolfo, I'm not married."

It took him a few minutes to recover. The pain that had stabbed at his heart lifted and he was able to smile.

She touched his hand, and a new ache shot through him. "I would love for you to come to America and visit Minnesota."

"How old is your daughter?"

"She's five."

His smile broadened across his face. "I come see her at right age. She old enough to not forget me."

She couldn't imagine anyone forgetting that they had met Rudolfo. She would always remember meeting him at the café. The way he looked, the way he sounded.

"We go in sitting room and relax. You tell me more about yourself and your daughter."

They sat down and at first just listened to the rain beating down against the windows. Francesca sipped her coffee, and Rudolfo watched her and saw loneliness in her eyes. The same loneliness he had felt before she'd come back to Florence, and he wanted to know more about her, and if they could help each other dispel their loneliness.

"Tell me about your daughter."

"She's very independent for her age. Her name is Annie. She has long brown curly hair."

"Like her mother."

"Yes. She's in kindergarten and she likes going to school and even does her homework."

"Where is her father?" asked Rudolfo—a little apprehensive of the answer, but he had to ask.

"She doesn't know her father. We never got married and he chose to leave when he found out I was pregnant. I regretted staying too long in a relationship that wasn't based on love, but I don't regret having Annie."

"Where she stay when you are traveling?"

"With her grandmother. They both enjoy spending time together. Sometimes too much," said Francesca, with a nervous laugh.

"What occupies your time besides work and Annie?"

She had to stop and think and finally said, "That's all."

"And you've become lonely."

It was a statement that was painfully true. Yes, she had become lonely. She worked hard and spent most of her time with Annie, never doing anything for herself. Yes, she was lonely, especially at night.

Rudolfo stood, took her cup, and set it on the end table. "Do you feel better about me after coming to my home?"

"Yes, much better. I don't know why I'm here, but I do feel better."

He looked out the window. "Do you want to go out?"

"No, I want to stay here with you."

"You have big travel day tomorrow. You sleep for a while. I go out and get something for dinner. The chair pulls out like recliner or you can lie on messy bed."

Francesca laughed. "It doesn't look messy to me."

"I go now. You sleep."

The night before she had imagined all sorts of things happening to her after meeting Rudolfo, and she hadn't been able to sleep. Her colleagues had told her to go ahead and meet with Rudolfo. Amy, a colleague and friend said she'd regret it later if she hadn't met with him. Now she was tired and sat back in the chair. Rudolfo shut the door quietly behind him.

Francesca closed her eyes and thought of Rob, Annie's father. He had been going to school to become an engineer, but his partying and drinking had been more important. He never took time to hold her or care for her the way she longed to be cared for. In the short time she'd known Rudolfo, he'd shown more concern than Rob ever had. On the rare occasion when Rob came home after class, they had sex. It was quick and unemotional, and afterward he would either fall asleep or leave again.

She had been disillusioned into thinking that's what love was all about. She knew differently now. But was it love she felt for Rudolfo? She would find out.

Chapter Two

He wanted to return sooner, but he met Filipo at the store, and his friend wanted the details of his visit with Francesca. He hurried back to his apartment, and his insides churned when Francesca wasn't in the chair. His heart fell to think she would leave. As he carried the groceries to the kitchen, he stopped when he saw her lying on his bed. She was on her side and her hair was flowing over the edge of the bed. She looked like an angel. Her green boots were on the floor.

He went to the kitchen and started putting things away. Thoughts of Francesca were ever present. "I see it started raining again," she said, stretching.

Startled, he looked up. "You look lovely, Francesca, when you sleeping." She felt her cheeks turning red. "No one tells you these things. I tell you."

"Come sit down, Rudolfo. It's your turn to tell me about you."

They returned once more to the sitting room. "Have you ever been married?" Francesca asked.

"I met someone while I was having lunch one day. She came into restaurant. I had finished my lunch and was sketching and drinking coffee. She very interested and asked me about my work. But after dating for several months she told me to quit and find decent job. She wanted me to get a job that would pay for her accustomed lifestyle, of not working and going to social functions."

"What did you tell her?"

"I told her no, and she left me." He looked away. "I was to marry once, but she left for America to be with someone else."

"How awful!"

He looked into her beautiful eyes. "It was good thing we not marry." Then, sheepishly, he added, "I want children and she didn't. It must've scared her."

"I'm sure it still hurt."

"It did. I put all my energy into my work after that."

"That's too bad, but I guess it's a good thing you found out." She paused. "What do you do for a living?"

"I'm a painter and a writer."

Francesca kept repeating his name, Rudolfo Vittori, in her mind. "You have books published!"

"You read them?" he asked, pleased.

"Several of them. The ones you wrote on the techniques of drawing and watercolor, but then you wrote something unexpected, an autobiography on what it was like to be an artist and a writer." She remembered she had read it twice. "I found it intriguing."

He was excited that she had read his books.

"I've not seen your paintings." She looked around the room. "Do you have any here?"

"Yes, in the room off the kitchen is my studio. I show you after dinner," he said. "What do you do, Francesca, that you work so hard?"

"I buy and sell leather goods. Since Florence has good quality leather, I come once a month to see what Italy's stores are selling." She elaborated a little more on working from home and going into the office only for meetings. "My company is fascinated by Italy's fashion."

"A long trip to see what Italy like to wear."

"I enjoy it." She thought of Annie wanting to come to Italy—her daughter would have no problem with browsing the clothing stores, and especially the shoe stores so far away. "Maybe someday Annie can come with me."

They talked several more hours until Rudolfo showed her his studio, and while she was looking at his paintings, he started dinner.

"Rudolfo!" cried Francesca from the studio. He came quickly and she turned around and gestured to all his works. "They're beautiful, so lifelike. You must spend hours capturing the right setting." She pointed to a painting that was hung on the wall, in an elegant-looking frame. "That's me, isn't it?"

"Yes. My finest work. It never be sold." This was said with such intensity that Francesca backed away from him. Staring at the picture, he said, "I spend many sleepless nights working on it." He turned to her and whispered, "Francesca."

He went to her and touched her cheek. "I ache for you, Francesca." As soon as he said it, he heard Filipo's voice, "not too fast, you scare her," and he dropped his hand. "I wish you not traveling tomorrow."

Feeling anxious, she backed away from him, and the room seemed to close in on her. She didn't see a viable path to get away from him. So instead she sat on the chair in the corner of the small room.

"I frightened you, Francesca." Tears came to his eyes. "I not mean to scare you."

She looked so pale. He wanted to go to her, but he felt he'd better stay where he was, at least until the color returned to her face. "I will not harm you, Signorina. I promise, believe me."

After failed attempts at taking a deep breath, she said in a weak voice, "I need to get out of here; the room is closing in on me."

His hand extended toward her, but she ignored it. He moved aside and she hurried past him to the sitting room and slumped in the recliner. He didn't want to scare her again, so he waited in the hall for several minutes.

He waited patiently for her to call to him and tell him what had happened. And then he smelled smoke, uttered something in Italian, and went to the stove and turned off the burner. He shook his head, "Ruined! What else can go wrong?!"

She was standing in the doorway to the kitchen. "Are you all right?" she asked, concerned he had gotten burned. But he didn't hear her.

He was sure she would go back to her hotel room. The pain he felt was intensified as he realized there was nothing he could do to stop her. After all, he had scared her.

After taking the kitchen towel, he lifted the cast iron frying pan off the stove and put it in the sink. While running the water he turned and noticed Francesca standing, watching him. He turned off the faucet.

Rudolfo looked at her. She still looked pale, and the emptiness he felt only increased.

"The room was so small I felt like you were going to hurt me." The images frightened her. "My boyfriend used to corner me and was very abusive, and that was all I could think of." Suddenly feeling weary, she sat down on the kitchen chair.

"Are you feeling better now?" He asked, sure that it was over between them.

"Once I left the room, I was fine." She looked at him. "I know I overreacted, but it all happened so fast." Feeling embarrassed now, she changed the subject. "I hope you're not just keeping your paintings in that room. That would be a shame."

"I sell many of them. I paint one for each of Carmella's children. She tells me what they like and I paint it for them." He sat next to her. "Antonio, her oldest, likes lighthouses. Carmella take me to Long Island and I paint his favorite one while he sit next to me and hand me the brushes. We had such a good time I long to have children of my own."

"What have you painted for her other children? There are six of them, right?"

"Yes, six of them." He smiled. "My sister love children." He took a minute to recall what he had painted for each of them.

"Caterina, her second child, want me to paint a horse she love to ride when they go into Pennsylvania. So we go there to paint." He looked at her and continued. "For Mario, her third child, I paint the beach. We walk and walk until he find just the right place."

"They've kept you busy on your visits. What about the rest of the children?"

"Franco, her fourth, want me to paint him. Only by the Statue of Liberty." Closing his eyes, he smiled. When he opened them again, he said, "Ah, and then there is Maria. We go to Bronx Zoo and I paint part of the Southeast Asian rainforest for her." Rudolfo smiled. "She right by my side making sure I paint it as we saw it."

"Giovanni, her youngest, say he keep it a surprise what he want me to paint. He not even told his mother."

"You could be in for quite an adventure."

He thought about that. "Carmella say every day is adventure with six children." He took Francesca's hand. "You not disappointed I ruin dinner?"

"No," she answered and then laughed. A smile came to his face.

"I take you out and have you back early to get good night's sleep before traveling. Put your boots on while I clean up."

She went to the bedroom, sat on the bed, and ran her fingers over the pillow. He's lonely, too, she thought. She knew she needed him in her life, but he lived so far away. She took his pillow and put it in her lap. Maybe we can help each other, she thought.

Rudolfo was watching her from the doorway, then came in and knelt down in front of her and put her boots on. She touched his face and he laid his head on the pillow. She stroked his hair. "Come to America before Christmas. We'll drive up north and you can sketch the snow clinging to the trees, the ice on the lakes, and the cabins that have been abandoned for the winter. We'll go to downtown Minneapolis and you can draw the skyscrapers."

She laid her head on his and started to outline his lips with her fingers. He hugged her legs to his body. He caught himself before he said, 'Francesca, you make me mad with passion.' "Francesca, we need to get away from bedroom."

"Then say you'll come sooner to America."

"I come, Francesca, as soon as you like. Now let me up before I . . ."

She moved closer to his lips and kissed him. "Rudolfo, I . . ." She sat up and he got to his feet and walked briskly down the hall to the door. He unlocked it. Francesca was behind him, and they left together.

Once outside, Rudolfo put his arm around her waist. "Are you cold, Francesca?"

"I'm still feeling quite warm, thank you."

They ate spaghetti, drank wine, and talked about the city. They shared their favorite museums and places to sit and watch people. Rudolfo told her about the place where he sat and sketched, and that sometimes he went to people's homes to paint portraits.

They both knew that the day would end soon, so they exchanged phone numbers. "I should get back to the hotel," said Francesca reluctantly. "I have an early flight and I'm not packed yet."

Rudolfo paid the bill and they walked back to the hotel. "I come, what you call Thanksgiving, no?"

"Yes! You can stay at my home. We have an extra bedroom downstairs."

"Will that be okay with Annie if I come?"

"Yes, she'll drive you crazy with her constant chatter."

"Ah, two lovely ladies to drive me crazy." The thought of it made him smile. "Will you kiss me again as before?"

She stared into his brown eyes and wondered how things between them had moved so quickly. She had met a man in a coffee shop and already he was coming to America to meet her daughter and stay in her home.

He couldn't wait for her to kiss him. So he kissed her. It was urgent and passionate. They knew they wouldn't see one another for several more weeks, so they put all their feeling into one kiss. He moved away from her, unsure of what he would do next. "Two lovely ladies in America, I come for sure. I call you when my ticket comes in mail."

"I can't wait to see you again."

"Arrivederci, Signorina."

"Till we meet again, Rudolfo."

She turned and walked slowly up the stairs. Rudolfo watched until she got to the top, then turned and walked home.

Chapter Three

"Rudy, you ready to travel tomorrow?"

"I ready for four weeks since Francesca left."

"Don't forget to see Carmella, she wonder where you are if you stay in Minnesota and not go to New York. Remember nephew, he five now."

"I won't forget. I ask Francesca, her mom, and Annie to come to Carmella's to celebrate Christmas when I in Minnesota."

"Does Carmella know?"

"Yes, I call her. She pleased."

"I know Carmella, she pleased you got a lady after all these years."

"She say that, too," said Rudolfo with humor in his voice.

"You don't forget to come back to Florence. I will miss you."

"I come back for visits," said Rudolfo, winking at his friend.

Filipo laughed. "You move fast, old friend. You come back. You live here. You miss Florence, she your first love."

"You know me too well," said Rudolfo. "You come to America to live with us."

His friend laughed again. "You always make me laugh. I never leave city, not even to visit."

"I write you. You write me?"

"Italian mail so slow, I send card for wedding and you not get until you have first child."

Rudolfo laughed, but he felt warm inside thinking about a wedding and a child.

"Get yourself computer, we keep in touch every day."

"No, no, no, I don't know how to work computers."

"I bet your lovely lady does. Here, you take my e-mail address." Rudolfo wrote it on a napkin then put it in his pocket.

"You tell her to send me message saying you arrive in America. Have safe trip, Rudy. I be here when you get back."

They embraced and said arrivederci.

*   *   *

"Annie, we are having a guest coming tonight, and he is going to stay with us for a month."

"That's a long time, Mom. Who is he? He's not my dad, is he?"

"No."

"Good." Annie offered no explanation for her answer, and Francesca wasn't going to ask.

"I met him in Florence, when I went to Italy last month."

"Grandma will be happy you have a new friend. She always tells me you should get out more and meet new people. Mostly she says you should meet men."

"She does, does she?"

"I agree with her, Mom. You don't do anything, except with me and Grandma. What's his name?"

"Rudolfo Vittori."

"I can't say that. I'll ask him if I can call him something else. If he's coming tonight, can I go to the airport with you?"

"I was hoping you would."

"I know he's a guest, but do I have to wear a dress?"

"No, your jeans are fine. His plane comes later, so you can go to school first."

"Darn," and she started to pout.

"You like school—why would you want to take the day off?"

"I like days off, too."

"Grandma said she would pick you up and take you to McDonald's after school. Then we can leave for the airport when you get home."

"Okay, I hope Rud . . . Rud . . . you know, likes me."

"I know he will. You can probably call him Rudy if you can't pronounce his name."

Francesca kissed and hugged her daughter good-bye and walked her out to the bus stop to wait with her and the other moms. After the bus came she went back to her office and tried working on an inventory report, but she couldn't concentrate.

Since she had left Florence, Rudolfo had been on her mind, and today she thought about him constantly. She turned off the computer and went upstairs. After pacing room after room, Francesca called her mother.

"Pick me up. I'm going stir crazy. Let's go shopping."

Francesca's mother laughed. She was used to her daughter's shopping sprees—although they hadn't been on one for over a year, Rose knew one was coming. The stress her daughter was going through worrying about Rudolfo coming to America was taking its toll on her. It was no surprise to get Francesca's phone call.

Francesca had called her mom as soon as she had returned from Florence, and it had been two in the morning. She'd talked non-stop until three. "Mom, I'm not sure what's happening, but it feels good and it feels right with Rudolfo," she had told Rose. There had been similar phone calls since, and Rose knew that her daughter would be heading to the stores sooner or later.

"I'll leave now, honey. Remember, I have to pick up Annie, so we can't do this all day."

"Okay, Mom, hurry."

*   *   *

"It's almost time to pick up Annie. Are you ready to go, Francesca?"

"Almost. I want to find a dress to wear when Rudolfo and I go out some night for dinner."

"Oh, honey. It sounds like he wasn't interested in your clothes, but in you."

"I know, Mom. I'm just nervous."

Rose put an arm around her daughter. "That black dress you tried on earlier was stunning on you. Let's go find it and then we can pick up Annie."

*   *   *

"I don't see him, Mom. Tell me again what he looks like."

"He has long hair like your friend Nicole's father has, but it's a little grayer, and he's tall like Mommy."

"Is he skinny like you, too?"

"Yes, but not as thin as Mommy."

"I still don't see him."

Francesca was holding Annie as they waited by the luggage carousel. Annie's questions had stopped and Francesca started reminiscing about when she had been in Rudolfo's apartment.

"Mom, are you sure he's coming?"

"He said he was." Noticing all of a sudden how heavy Annie was getting in her arms, she walked over to a row of chairs and they sat down. They were still close enough to the carousel that they could see everyone. After all the luggage had been claimed and no one was left standing around, Annie spoke.

"He must've missed the plane, Mom."

Dread washed over Francesca. How could she have been such a fool and believed he would come to Minnesota? He had sounded sincere. And then there was the painting of her in his small studio. How would she tell Annie that she'd made a huge mistake and, worse yet, how would she explain it to her mother?

In a shaky voice, she said, "Let's go home, Annie."

"Maybe he's on the next flight, and just missed this one."

She felt a surge of hope that there was some truth in what her daughter said, but she chided herself again for thinking he would come. "Let's go home. I'm tired, and you have to get to bed, too."

Sensing her sadness, Annie wrapped her arms around her mother's neck.

On the way home from the airport, Annie was soon fast asleep, buckled in her seat belt in the back seat, leaving Francesca to her thoughts.

Going over and over in her mind how she would tell her mom about the mistake she'd made, Francesca developed a stomachache. She tried to calm herself and wondered if she should call Rudolfo. He had left her a phone number where he could be reached. That's what she would do. Get Annie in bed, call Rudolfo, and then she would have a plausible story for her mother.

Annie willingly went to bed once they arrived home. Rudolfo's phone rang several times. She wanted to leave a message, but an answering machine never came on. As soon as she had hung up, the phone rang. Maybe he had caller ID, she thought.

"Francesca, did Rudolfo have a safe trip?"

Anxiety washed over her. "No."

"What happened? Were there plane problems?"

"No. He didn't come."

"I don't understand. He said he was coming . . . and didn't?"

"I just called him and no one answered. I probably got the information wrong. Who knows, he might be at the airport right now waiting for me." She paused, "Or he never intended to come."

"I saw the letter, too, and you got the information right." Rose sighed. "There is probably a good explanation."

"When it comes to men, they always have a good explanation . . . for not being with me."

"Don't be so hard on yourself."

"I can't help it. Not seeing Rudolfo tonight made me realize just how naive I am."

There was silence, and then Rose spoke. "In his letter he mentioned his friend. Was there a phone number?"

"What good is that going to do?"

"You can call him and find out what happened."

"I don't care anymore. I'm done. If he really wanted to come and see us he would've been on the plane, or at least he would've called."

"Don't be like that. Not all men are like Annie's father." Rose wished she were there so she could shake her daughter. "Do you have his sister's number in New York?"

"No." Suddenly feeling tired, Francesca said, "I'm going to bed. I'll deal with it in the morning."

"Be prepared to start answering questions from Annie. She was looking forward to seeing him, and I don't think she'll give up as easily as you have."

"Oh, thanks . . . for all your support." She pulled Rudolfo's letter from her purse. "I'll call him again tomorrow."

"Promise?"

Hesitantly, Francesca repeated the word, "Promise." Then hung up.

She read the letter again. It said that Rudolfo would be in Minneapolis on this day and at the time she was at the airport. She didn't understand what could've happened. She put her nightgown on, checked on Annie, and went to bed.

The next morning Rose let herself in, made breakfast, and was hoping that Annie wouldn't bombard her with all sorts of questions about the evening before.

Annie shoveled scrambled eggs into her mouth. "I think Mom's friend just forgot." She gulped down some milk. "I forgot to go to Grace's house one time." Picking up her bacon and biting off a piece, she continued, "She called me and asked me where I was and then she got mad at me. But we're friends now. Mom just needs to call him again."

Ah! The innocence of a child. If life were that easy, thought Rose. She picked up Annie's dishes and brought them to the counter by the sink.

"Mom?" Rose turned. "Thanks for coming." Francesca bent down, kissed Annie on the cheek, and sat down next to her. "I'm at a loss as to what to do. I called again last night fairly late and no one answered." She looked at her mother, and Rose knew what she was implying.

"No, Francesca, he wasn't home and just didn't answer your call. I feel as if something has happened." She added more dishes to the dishwasher. "We need to contact his friend."

Francesca dug into her robe pocket, pulled out the letter and smoothed down the edges on the table. Annie knelt on her chair and looked at the letter with her mom. Annie turned it over. "Is that it?" she asked as she pointed to a phone number.

"Yes, it's Filipo's number." Francesca was counting and Annie giggled at her. "It's seven hours difference in Italy, so I was trying to figure out what time it was there," Francesca said.

Annie looked at the clock, pointed, and moved her finger around in a circle as she counted off seven hours. "It's four o'clock there!" She straightened up in her chair. "I think we should call him right now." She leaped out of the chair, brought the phone and set it in front of her mother.

Rose had a grin on her face. "Well, are you going to call?"

Annie picked up the phone. "You read the numbers and I'll punch them in."

Francesca slowly read off the numbers and when she'd read off the last one, Annie handed her the phone. The phone rang. He won't be there, she thought. Or if he is, he won't know where Rudolfo is, or worse, he'll laugh at me for being so gullible. After the tenth ring she hung up.

She felt a hand on her arm. "We'll try again later, Mom. Can I go outside and play?"

"Sure, but first I need a hug." Annie wrapped her arms around her mother and squeezed her as hard as she could. "Are you feeling better now, Mom?"

"Much better."

"I'll come and check on you after I play outside for a while." She walked to the back door and told her grandmother to follow her. Then Annie said, "Let's take Mom to that restaurant on Johnson Street for supper tonight." Annie took her jump rope off the hook. "That's her favorite. She likes to order those messy burgers."

Rose put her hand on Annie's shoulder and looked straight at her. "That's an excellent idea. We should go early before the crowd."

"Okay, Grandma, I'm going outside now."

Chapter Four

Annie's friend Grace came over and they were in the playhouse most of the morning. Rose told Francesca about the plans for dinner, then went home.

Amy, Grace's mother, had been there for Francesca when she was dating Rob. Amy had tried to talk her into leaving the abusive relationship soon after they had started dating, but Francesca was sure he would change. When he didn't, she thought, she was too far into the relationship to get out.

When she found out that she was pregnant with Annie, Amy convinced her to leave Rob. However, she didn't have to make the decision. Once Rob found out she was pregnant, he left on his own. She needed to talk to Amy again, but felt too embarrassed by what had happened.

Now Francesca just wanted to go back to bed, but instead she took a shower and put on jeans and a sweatshirt. Periodically she looked out to check on Annie. The leaves had turned, and most of the trees were bare. There was a chill in the air. Next week would be Thanksgiving. Rudolfo wanted to be here to celebrate with us. Did he really? she asked herself. Shaking her head, she went downstairs and turned on the computer. Working would be a way to keep her mind off Rudolfo. But thoughts of their first meeting and the day she had spent with him kept flooding into her mind.

The more she tried to concentrate, the more she couldn't. In frustration, she turned off the computer, went outside, and knocked on the playhouse door.

"What's the password?"

"Alligator." The two little girls giggled, and Grace opened the door.

"Mom, we changed the password, but we'll let you in this time." Annie cleared off a small chair for Francesca to sit on. "The new password. Oh, wait! We have to do the swearing-in so you promise not to tell anyone."

Francesca smiled. She had been through the same ritual several times before. They all stood, held hands, and closed their eyes. Grace did the ritual this time. She chanted, "Mrs. Jones, will you swear never to tell the password or the location of our private clubhouse? You will be. . ."

Annie interjected, "secre . . .tive about our meetings and members."

Finishing, Grace continued, "Do you swear, Mrs. Jones?"

"Yes, I fully swear never to tell."

They walked around in a circle while holding hands, stopped and went in the opposite direction, then stopped again. They held up their hands, and then Annie shook her mother's hand. "Welcome into our club."

Grace wrote something on a piece of paper, folded the paper, and handed it to Francesca. "You can open this only in a dark place where no one can see you. Do you swear?"

"Yes, I do."

"Okay, Mom, that's it." Annie sat down in her chair, the one reserved for the club president. It was painted red, with flowers and a few stickers adorning the legs. Grace took the chair for members only. This one was painted sky blue, with no flowers and no stickers. The third chair, the one Francesca sat in, was painted yellow. It had no other distinguishing feature except that the legs were uneven.

"What's up, Mom? Do you want to hang out with us for a while?"

"I just wanted to come out and see if you were okay, and it looks like you are."

"Grace has to go home in thirty minutes. Then we can hang out."

Francesca stood, did the official handshake, and left. After walking into her bedroom, the darkest room in the house, she opened the folded piece of paper. Tears welled in her eyes. "Rudy" was scribbled on the paper.

She curled up on the bed and clutched the paper to her chest. Where did she go wrong? What could she have done better? When he had last called, they had had a pleasant conversation, both anxious to see each other again. He especially wanted to see Annie and to meet her mother.

The phone rang and she jumped. Was it him?

"Hello."

"Franny, is your mother there?"

"No, June, she went home over an hour ago."

"She told me all about your friend. How are Annie and he getting along?"

After pausing for several seconds, she answered. "He didn't make it."

"Oh, I'm sorry to hear that. Well, I was just trying to reach Rose. She seems to have disappeared." There was a laugh on the other end. "She's probably out in her garden getting ready for the freeze that's coming." Silence. "Tell her I called."

"I will." She hung up the phone. Now the whole world will know what a mistake I made.

Annie was standing there, watching her. "I'm ready to hang out." Annie sat next to Francesca on the bed. "Grace thinks you're cool. Her mom never plays with her. When you see Amy, again, tell her to play with Grace."

"I think Grace is cool, too, and I'll tell Amy."

"Let's call Rudy's friend again."

Before Francesca could say no, Annie was pulling her hand and leading her into the kitchen. She sat Francesca down and brought her the phone.

"I guess I can't say no, can I?" Francesca said.

"Nope!" They went through the routine—Annie punching in the numbers as Francesca read them off.

This time Annie kept the phone and counted each ring out loud. When she got to ten, she looked at her mom. Francesca mouthed, "Hang up."

After hanging up, Annie said, "We'll try again in the morning. Hey, did you try Rudy? I think we should call him now." She picked up the phone. "Okay, I'm ready."

Again, no answer from Rudolfo. That he wasn't coming was one thing, but the anticipation of his answering his phone was almost more than Francesca could bear. She wanted to move on, to write this chapter off as another bad decision. And yet she felt something for him. She had felt it would be different this time and had sensed that he was sincere, and most of all, trustworthy, unlike anyone she had met before.

After leaving Florence, she'd thought of him often, and loved to talk about him with her mother. She hadn't told Annie the whole story, only mentioned that she had met somebody while working in Italy.

"Mom! Aren't you listening?"

Pulled from her thoughts, she answered, "What, honey?"

"Come on," Annie said. She took Francesca's hand again and led her to the bedroom. "Take a nap and I'll wake you up when Grandma gets here to take us to eat." She pulled the blanket off the chair in the corner. "I'll cover you. I know you are sad, Mom, so if you sleep you won't have to think about Rudy anymore."

Francesca smiled to herself. She was tired, and a good nap just might solve everything.

*   *   *

"I'll order for everyone," said Annie when the waiter came to their table. They always ordered the same thing; still Annie had the menu open in front of her. Rose had taught her how to read not too long ago, but instead she pointed to the pictures as she ordered. "We want three of these burgers, two of these kinds of fries. My mom wants water. My grandma wants coffee with cream, and I want chocolate milk."

"Is that all, young lady?" asked the waiter.

"Oh, and we want dessert menus when we're done eating."

"Dessert?" asked Rose and Francesca in unison.

"It's a special occasion." Annie looked at the waiter and handed him the menus. He left to put in their order.

"What's the occasion? We never order dessert," said Francesca.

Annie pushed the curls away from her face. Sitting on her feet with her elbows on the table, she was coloring her placemat. "Rudy's coming!" She stopped coloring. "They had this picture last time," she said, then continued coloring.

Her mother and grandmother looked at each other. "It must be true if she said it with such conviction." Rose looked at her daughter, "I hope you believe it, too."

Francesca didn't know what to believe. She had prepared for Rudolfo's arrival ever since she had left Florence. But would she ever hear from him again?

When they were finished eating, the waiter dropped off dessert menus as requested. When he came back, Annie pointed to the chocolate cake. "My mom wants this, and my grandma wants the lemon cake."

"What would you like?" he asked her.

"Do you have cookies?"

"We don't have them listed, but the chef just made some. She thought we could eat them on our break." He wrote something down on his pad. "Do you like chocolate chip?"

"Yummy."

He took the menus, "I'll be right back."

*   *   *

When they got home, the answering machine was blinking. Francesca ignored it. Not ready for any bad news, she went to her bedroom to change into her nightgown.

"Hey, Grandma, you have to push the button," Annie said to Rose. "I accidentally erased a message one time and Mom said I couldn't check it anymore."

Rose wasn't so sure she wanted to do it either. What if her daughter was right—if it was all a joke and he was calling to tell her that?

"Come on, Grandma. You have to push the button."

Rose moved closer to the cupboard. Several long seconds passed, then she pushed the button.

"Francesca," said the voice in a strong Italian accent. "Rudy . . . not coming—" The rest of the message was cut off and the phone disconnected.

"I told you," Francesca said. Both Annie and Rose turned to look at her. "He's not coming."

"Call Filipo back and find out why. Don't just assume you know what's happened," Rose said.

"It's two o'clock in the morning in Italy. I'll wait until tomorrow."

*   *   *

Rudolfo's friend was mopping his fevered brow with a wet cloth. "Hang in there. You'll get better." Rudolfo could only respond with a moan. Since he'd been in the hospital, he kept fading in and out of consciousness. A woman was on his mind and every time he got close to her she would fade into the darkness.

His fever was high for a man his age. His doctor had put him in the hospital for observation and had done numerous tests. They still hadn't figured out why he was so restless.

*　　*　　*

At three in the morning, Francesca called both phone numbers, Rudolfo's and Filipo's. No one answered. She tried to go back to sleep, and when that didn't work she went to the couch and tried to read. But her thoughts wouldn't let her be at peace.

When Filipo had left the message, it sounded as though he had had a hard time getting the words out. What had happened to Rudolfo? she wondered. There was no way she could find out if no one answered the phone. Then a thought came to her. She ran downstairs and turned on the computer. She looked up hospitals in Florence, wrote the names down, went back upstairs, took the phone, and sat at the kitchen table.

She dialed the first hospital on her list. "No," came the reply to her question. After calling the second one on the list, she got the same answer. She put the phone down and stared at the last number on the list. If he's not there, she thought, she would forget this whole thing, forget Rudolfo, and forbid Annie and Rose to talk about him ever again. Reluctantly she dialed.

"Is Rudolfo Vittori at the hospital?"

"Yes," came the woman's reply, after several seconds. "Do you want to talk to him?"

"What room is he in?"

The receptionist gave her the room number and asked again, "Do you want to talk to him . . . Miss., are you there?"

"Yes, I would like to talk to him."

"I'll connect you."

"Hello."

"Rudolfo?"

"No, this is Filipo." There was silence on the line.

"This is Francesca." She took a Kleenex and wiped her eyes. "Is . . . is Rudolfo all right?"

"No. He has a fever."

"Is he able to talk?" She longed to hear his voice, to figure out some logical order to this whole thing. Now more than ever she wanted to see him, to feel his kiss, his touch, and to hear his thick Italian accent.

"Francesca, he can't talk. He keeps falling in and out of sleep. The only thing he says is your name." He took the cloth and blotted his friend's forehead. "I know once the fever goes down he'll be upset he missed his trip."

"I just want him well. Please keep me informed about his progress." She held back the urge to cry, and continued. "Call me anytime, day or night."

"I call. I get him on plane, too, when he well. All he does is talk about you, and now he sick and still he say your name. He got it bad, Francesca."

Nothing that could've been said would have been such music to her ears. "Tell him when he wakes up that I love him."

They said good-bye, and she hung up. She was happy that she had found out about Rudolfo and a weight had lifted from her body, but now she worried about his health. Would it be a good idea to go to Florence to be with him? She would wait until her next call from Filipo to see if she should go.

She felt exhausted and decided to go back to bed. Rudolfo was on her mind, but now she knew where he was. Sleep came easier than it had the last two nights.

*   *   *

"Mommy, get up, you have to take me to school. I missed the bus." Annie shook her mom again and hoped this time she would wake up. "Mom, get up."

Francesca moved and looked at her daughter. "It can't be a school day, can it?"

"Yep, it can."

She moved slowly as she got out of bed. "Are you sure it's a school day?" She winked at Annie. "You don't want to play hooky."

"Mom, I can't believe you said that." She pulled her mom's hand as Francesca got out of bed, and led her to the bathroom. "Get dressed, you have five minutes."

"Now you sound like me."

"I'll go down and make breakfast. Don't fool around, either, Mom. I don't want to be late."

In five minutes Francesca walked into the kitchen and sat down. Cereal was poured into bowls, milk was on the table, and coffee was made.

"When did you learn how to make coffee?"

"Grandma showed me. You'll have to pour your own. I don't want to get burned."

They ate their cereal. Francesca poured coffee into her travel mug and secured the lid. "I'm ready, let's go." She helped Annie with her jacket. "I have news about Rudolfo, I'll tell you on the way to school."

"Is he going to be all right?" asked Annie after her mother told her about Rudolfo. "I knew something happened, otherwise he would be here already. Are you going to be okay today?" She took her backpack off the floor. "You've been so sad since we went to the airport. Maybe Grandma can take you shopping. I know that will cheer you up."

Francesca stopped in front of the school. She kissed her daughter good-bye and watched as she ran to meet Grace.

*　　*　　*

Francesca returned home, called her mother and told her about Rudolfo. Rose said, "I hate to say I told you so."

"You are always right, Mom. I should listen to you more often."

"Now what are you going to do about Rudolfo?"

"I'm going to wait for another call about his progress."

"That's a good idea, but don't wait too long."

*　　*　　*

Two days later she called the hospital. "He went home this morning," said the nurse. Francesca hung up, then dialed Rudolfo's number. An answering machine came on, and after the recording stopped, she hung up in frustration. The recording was of a woman's voice, asking the caller to please leave a message for Rudolfo. Panic swept through her. Did he move, was he avoiding her? She dialed several more times and got the same thing, then slammed down the phone. "Now what?!" she asked herself. She let out a scream in hopes it would make the situation more bearable. "Now what?!" she repeated.

After walking to the closet and getting what she needed, she filled the bucket with water, then started to mop the kitchen floor. She kept mopping the same spot over and over again as thoughts went through her mind. This is it. I'm not calling ever again. If I hear from him I'll just tell him it's over, it's been too stressful, and I don't want to see him ever again.

The phone was ringing, but Francesca didn't hear it. She kept mopping the floor. Kept thinking about what a fool she was. It wasn't until she heard a man's voice that she stopped what she was doing and stared at the phone. All she heard was ". . . your call" and the sound of hanging up.

It was Rudolfo. Tears flooded down her cheeks. She was too startled to move. She watched as Annie took the phone and sat down at the table. "Mom, let's call him back." She pushed a button and replayed the message. "Francesca, I home. I wait for your call."

Annie picked up the letter from the table and starting dialing. "No!" cried Francesca. She put the mop back into the bucket, walked out of the kitchen, and slammed her bedroom door.

Annie disconnected, and then proceeded to call her grandmother. "Grandma, Mom isn't doing well. Rudy left a message and she won't call him back. Can you come over?"

"Sure, I'll be right there."

*　　*　　*

Francesca wasn't sure why she had reacted the way she had. It had taken everything she had out of her when she'd heard the woman's voice on Rudolfo's answering machine. After sitting on her bed for a while, she decided she wanted to talk to him, to hear his voice. He sounded good, not sick the way he had been two days earlier. Most of all, she wanted to see him. Thanksgiving was five days away, and she wanted him to be there. She took a shower and pulled on some jeans and a raggedy sweatshirt, then went to the kitchen. Rose and Annie were playing cards. They looked up when she entered the room.

"Annie tells me that you don't want to speak to Rudolfo again," said Rose. She laid a card on Annie's pile. "Tell me what's going on."

Francesca sat and folded her arms. "When he wasn't at the airport I felt betrayed, and since it wasn't a new feeling with men, I had a hard time dealing with it." She watched Annie. "I'm ready to call him back now. I want him here. Getting sick wasn't his fault, and he wasn't lying to me. I realize that now. I'm so used to men lying to me that I got a little crazy."

"A little crazy," repeated Annie as she shuffled the cards.

"Come here, you. I need a hug." Annie went into her arms and gave her a squeeze. "I feel much better now," Francesca said.

Annie reached over, took the phone off the table, and handed it to her mother. "Then call him, before he thinks you are be . . . be . . . traying him."

Annie got down and Francesca dialed from memory. She was ready to hang up on the sixth ring when Rudolfo answered, out of breath. "Hello."

"It's me, Francesca." She picked up a playing card and rubbed it with her thumb. "I called earlier, but an answering machine came on and it was a woman's voice."

"I had an answering service take my messages. I was waiting for an important call and I wanted to make sure I got the message, but mostly I didn't want to miss your call." There was silence. "You were worried. I realize now how it feel to hear woman's voice." More silence. "I sorry Francesca, I cause you pain."

She put the card down. "How are you feeling?"

"Better. But not enough to travel. I won't be there for Thanksgiving, but I try for week after. Travel won't be crowded then. Is that okay?"

"No, it's not okay. It's wonderful! She whispered, "I love you." As she hung up she looked at Annie. Her daughter had a big smile on her face. "Are you happy now, Mom?"

*   *   *

They didn't celebrate Thanksgiving. They were waiting for their guest, the one they were sure would show up this time, and would celebrate with him.

Chapter Five

"Mommy! Mommy! Is that him?"

Francesca was looking in the direction her daughter was pointing and looked right at Rudolfo. She smiled at him in his winter coat and scarf. Although Francesca felt like running up to him, she put Annie down, took her daughter's hand, and walked slowly over to him.

He put his arms around her. "Francesca, I miss you."

There was tugging on his pant leg, and he looked down. "I'm Annie." Annie held out her hand.

He bent down and kissed her hand, "I'm Rudolfo."

"Can I call you something else? I can't say your name."

"My good friend Filipo calls me Rudy."

"Rudy. I can say that! You look just like Mommy said you would. Mom has your room all ready. I dusted for you and picked up my toys. I fluffed up the pillows, too."

"Annie," said Francesca in a gentle voice. "Let's get Rudolfo's luggage. Then we can go home."

"Okay," said Annie. Then she grabbed Rudolfo's hand and started walking with him to the baggage area. She was quiet while Rudolfo explained what his luggage looked like. Then she stood close to the carousel and studied every piece that came down the chute.

"Francesca, you have lovely daughter." He put his arm around her as they watched Annie.

"Rudy! There it is, coming down the slide."

Rudolfo walked over and picked it up. "Yes, this is the one. Thank you, Annie." They walked to the parking lot, and Annie chattered all the way to the car. When Rudolfo could get Francesca's attention he smiled, then winked at her.

On the way home, Annie fell asleep in the back seat. "Filipo wanted to take me to the airport a couple of days early, I so anxious to see you. But I got sick. Francesca, I miss you so much."

"I missed you, too. How are you feeling?"

He took her hand and held it tightly. "I'm feeling fine, as if I was never sick." He looked at her. "We not be away from each other anymore."

She didn't know why he said he didn't want to be away from her since his plans were to go to New York two days before Christmas and then return to Florence after New Year's.

Since she wasn't sure she wanted to know why he had said it, she changed the subject. "Annie and I have planned a sightseeing tour for you while you are here in Minnesota. You can sit and sketch the sights."

"Yes, I like to go sightseeing."

"It's going to get colder by the end of next week, so we'll try and do as much as we can before then."

"It gets colder than this?" asked Rudolfo, with a worried look on his face.

"Yes, Rudolfo, much colder."

*　　*　　*

"My pajamas are on, but do I have to go to bed so early? Tomorrow we are pretending it's Thanksgiving and it's Saturday, too, right, Mom?"

"That's right," said Francesca, "but I want you to go to bed early, it's been a long day."

"But we have a guest. I should stay up and keep him company."

"Rudolfo had a long trip—he probably wants to go to bed, too."

Annie started to pout, and Rudolfo said, "I'll tuck you in, and then I'll go to bed, too, if that's all right with your mom."

"Can he, Mom, can he?"

"Sure, come here." Annie went to her mom and gave her a hug and then went down the hall with Rudolfo.

*   *   *

After saying goodnight to Annie, he walked over to Francesca. "She is a good little girl, Francesca." He put his hands on her shoulders and looked into her eyes. "I kiss you, no?"

"You kiss me, yes." Their arms went around each other and they kissed. His lips were stirring passion inside of her. Passion that had been hidden and now wanted to come out, to be released with this man, this stranger.

His fingers played with her hair as they kissed. Francesca put her hand on his chest. He let out a groan and backed away from her. "Will Annie wake up?" asked Rudolfo, out of breath.

"Yes, she could. Let me show you to your room."

Rudolfo took his suitcase and followed her down the stairs to the bedroom. There was a queen-sized bed with an old-fashioned quilt of greens and blues. "The closet is over there. The basement was made into a small apartment in hopes my mom would move in with us. But she's too independent. You can use anything you want. My office is on the opposite end."

"Too much space for me, Francesca." He waved his hands around the room. "This bigger than apartment in Florence."

She went over to him and they continued what they had started upstairs. Their kiss was more urgent this time. She hadn't been able to picture him in any setting except in his hometown of Florence, but he was here, in her home, kissing her passionately.

He wanted her. Now! The last month had been worse than those he'd spent tirelessly looking for her on the bridge. He had been sick and couldn't get to her. The dark nights had driven him crazy wanting her. Now he was here, and his body ached for her.

His lips parted and his tongue explored her mouth. Her hands started to explore his body, and when she felt she needed more of him she heard "Mommy."

Startled, they stepped back from each other and stared at the doorway. Annie was there rubbing her eyes. "I couldn't sleep. We didn't really have supper, only a snack after school at McDonald's."

Francesca moved over to her, picked her up, and faced Rudolfo, who was still trying to calm his senses. "Are you hungry, Rudy?" asked Annie.

Looking at his watch, he said, "At home at this time I have tea and a pastry."

"We have cookies and milk. Can we have some, Mommy?"

She couldn't resist her daughter, or Rudolfo's smile. "Okay, but then you both have to go to bed and stay there."

"I promise." She reached her arms out to Rudolfo. He took her and started walking up the stairs. Annie said, "Mommy, you can have cookies with us, too."

"I'll be up in a minute." She watched them climb the stairs and noticed how well they got along with one another. Although Annie was not shy, it usually took her a while to warm up to someone she'd just met. As unexplainable as it was, she loved Rudolfo Vittori.

As she got closer she could hear the chatter coming from the kitchen.

"You talk funny, Rudy."

"I have Italian accent."

"Teach me some Italian words."

"I teach you one. It's late and your mommy want you in bed." He looked at her. "Buon giorno. You can use it anytime during the day for good afternoon, good day, and good morning."

It took a little practice for Annie to get the pronunciation right. While Rudolfo was helping her, Annie didn't notice her mother walking into the kitchen, but Rudolfo was fully aware of her presence. Her jeans clung to her slim hips in a sensual way that made it hard for Rudolfo to concentrate on the Italian lesson he was giving.

"In the morning you say buon giorno when you get up. Now you go to bed again," said Francesca.

"Goodnight, Mommy. When did you get in the kitchen?"

"Before the Italian lesson."

She crawled down from Rudolfo's lap and went to bed.

"I can make you some tea," Francesca said to Rudolfo.

"Yes, I would like some."

He watched her fill the teakettle with water and get the tea down from the cupboard. She looked tired. He had the urge to get his sketch pad and draw her as she was standing at the stove, but he couldn't stop watching her.

They made small talk about Rudolfo's flight and about Carmella and his nieces and nephews while they drank their tea and ate too many cookies.

"It's late, Rudolfo, you must be exhausted."

"I am exhausted, but being with you keep me awake. Of all times I come to America, I have no idea a lovely lady live here in Minnesota."

"Go to bed, Rudolfo. You can tuck your own self in," laughed Francesca.

He reached for her hand, "Are you still afraid of me?"

"No. Not of you, but of how you make me feel. We need to get to know each other better. Be friends first."

The thought of making love to her was staggering. He held her hand tightly. "Francesca."

"You're whispering again."

He smiled at her, released her hand, and stood up. "I may never sleep if you not kiss me again and give me something to dream about."

"I have a feeling your dreams are already filled with me."

She went into his arms and they kissed, both anticipating that the voice of a child might interrupt. When none came, the kiss grew more intense.

She pushed away from him. "You must be tired. Go downstairs and get some sleep. We'll see each other in the morning."

Reluctantly he went downstairs and Francesca went to her own room.

Chapter Six

After a restless night, Rudolfo woke early, dressed, and went to the kitchen. He noticed the tea that Francesca had left out from the night before and put water on to boil. There was a noise at the back door, then suddenly it opened. A lady in her early fifties walked through the door with a bag of groceries, and was startled to see Rudolfo at the stove.

"Good morning. I'm Rose, Francesca's mother."

"Yes, yes." He took her hand and kissed it. "Buon giorno, Rose, I'm Rudolfo."

He looked just as Francesca had described him, and she had described him to her many times. She even described his tweed jacket that he was now wearing, the one that he had worn when Francesca met him. Rose had not been sure about his long graying hair, but seeing him, she thought he wore it well.

"I see you made it safely."

"Yes, long flight, but safe. Would you like tea?"

"No, thank you. That's all decaf. I'm going to make coffee. I need a lot of caffeine to wake up." She moved toward the cupboard. "How are you feeling? You gave us a big scare."

"Doctor not sure what to do, but I feel much better." He looked at Rose. "Much better now that I'm here with your daughter."

Rose was as tall as Francesca, observed Rudolfo. Her short, brown hair had red highlights and was swept away from her face. Francesca had her deep-set blue eyes.

Rose made coffee, then started to look around the kitchen.

"What you look for?"

"The pies Francesca was supposed to make last night so I can use the oven for the turkey."

"She not make pies last night."

"Well, I'm going to wake her up so she can make them now."

"No, no, she sleep. She tired. I make pies. You tell me what kind you want."

Rose had her doubts he could make anything, but she decided to let him try. "I'll get the recipe and all the ingredients."

After the ingredients were on the counter, she watched Rudolfo as she made preparations for their special Thanksgiving dinner. The pie crust was rolled once and put all in one piece into the pie tin. Rose was impressed. The ingredients were mixed and scraped into the pie crust. One was pumpkin, and one was pecan.

They were made with such ease, she was glad her daughter wasn't up to make them. It would've taken Francesca over an hour just to make the crust.

"Rudolfo, where did you learn to make pies?"

"My family have a bakery. We make pastries and pies all the time. I learn young."

"I'm glad we let Francesca sleep. The pies wouldn't be as good if she made them," said Rose with a laugh.

"Did I hear my name?"

"Buon giorno, Signorina. You look lovely, even in the morning."

Rose could see the color rise in her daughter's cheeks. "Buon giorno, Rudolfo. You look funny in the morning with flour all over your face."

"I make pies for you, so you not hear your mother raise her voice when she say your name."

Francesca laughed. "Thank you, Rudolfo."

"Where's Annie?" asked Rose.

"She's still sleeping. We stayed up late drinking milk and eating cookies."

Rose finished preparing the turkey, joined Rudolfo and Francesca at the table, and drank her coffee. "Francesca tells me you have a sister in New York and you visit whenever one of her children turns five."

"So far I been able to visit each one. She didn't say she have so many, though. Now I see Annie, she's five."

Rudolfo felt a tapping on his arm and looked down.

"Buon...ga no, Rudy."

"Buon giorno, Annie."

As Rose got up to get cereal and milk for her granddaughter, Annie started to climb into Rudolfo's lap. "Annie, sit over here. You don't need to sit on Rudolfo," said Francesca.

"Can I, Rudy, please?"

"Sure, you can," said Rudolfo, helping her into his lap.

Rose noticed how comfortable Annie was around Rudolfo, as if she'd known him her whole life.

"Mom, the batteries in my IPod need fixing. They don't work anymore."

"It sounds like you need to change them," said Francesca. "Do you have any extra batteries?"

"No," said Annie. She shoveled in another spoonful of cereal, and milk ran down her chin. "The store down the block has batteries. I know how to get there myself," she said in a grown-up voice as she scraped the bottom of the bowl for the last bit of cereal.

"I won't let you go alone, Annie," said her mother.

"Rudy can go with me."

"I go with you. You show me the way."

Annie pushed her empty bowl away and got down from Rudolfo's lap. "I'll be dressed in a minute," she said and ran out of the kitchen.

"She likes you, Rudolfo. She doesn't sit on anyone's lap," declared Rose.

Rudolfo smiled, "She a good girl. I like her, too."

Annie was back in the kitchen fully dressed with her winter jacket on. Rudolfo took his jacket from the hook by the door and they went outside.

"He's a quiet man, Francesca. They make good lovers."

"Mother!"

"He's a very loving man, kind, sweet. The traits of an intense lover."

"Mother!"

Rose kept talking despite the shock she heard in her daughter's voice. "Your father has been dead for years. I've dated since then, and I know from experience. He's good with Annie, too. She needs a father figure in her life, and Rudolfo would be perfect." Then, Rose continued to get a rise out of her daughter, "He will be an exceptional lover."

"Mother, stop it!" Francesca put her hands over her ears.

Rose laughed and went to check on the pies.

"You can't tell me when he kisses you, you don't feel all the passion he has. I can see it every time he looks at you."

"I'm not saying a word. The one thing I was worried about was that you wouldn't approve of him, but I can see I didn't have a thing to worry about."

"Why don't you go take a shower and get dressed? The pies will be done soon, and I'll put in the turkey. When you're done getting dressed, you can help with the rest of the meal."

"Thanks, Mom."

*   *   *

The smells of Thanksgiving were in the air. Everyone enjoyed the day and the food. They especially enjoyed the pies. Rudolfo taught Annie more Italian and had Rose reciting the phrases with Annie.

Around eight o'clock, Rudolfo announced that he would make tea and coffee and cut more pie. Rose groaned, she was so full, but said she wanted more pie anyway.

Annie went to bed after she had her pie and milk, and Rose put on her coat.

"Thanks, Mom, for all your help."

"Help! You helped, I did most of the work." Rose smiled at her daughter and then at Rudolfo.

"Thanks, Mom, for doing all the work," Francesca said, laughing. "We were going up north tomorrow, but we're supposed to have a snowstorm, so we might wait until Monday."

"Let me know," Rose said. She turned to Rudolfo. "Rudolfo, it was good to meet you. Next week I'll have everyone over to my house for dinner. You can come early, Rudolfo, and make more pies."

"I come." He extended his hand, and when Rose took it, he kissed her hand. "It was good to meet Francesca's mother." Rose smiled.

Rose left, and Rudolfo and Francesca sat back down at the table. Rudolfo took Francesca's hand and stared at it for a while before looking into her eyes. "I glad I come. You have nice family."

"Mom likes you very much, Rudolfo." Francesca felt warm thinking of what her mother had said—"good lover, intense lover."

If Francesca went by how much she knew about him, he would be a casual acquaintance, not someone she wanted to touch every time he was in the room.

"Annie likes you too. She'll be sad when you leave."

"You, Annie, Rose, come with me to New York for Christmas. Carmella want to meet you."

"She's already got a big family to care for. Would she want three more people?"

"Yes, she already invite you in a letter she send to Italy."

"It would be Annie's first plane ride. She's very curious about how planes stay in the air and what the inside of one looks like."

"Then she find out when we fly to New York."

"Yes, I want to go, Rudolfo. We'll ask Annie in the morning and I'll call Mom after that and ask her, too."

"That make me happy, Francesca. You make me happy."

He stood and pulled Francesca into his arms. In a whisper, he said, "Francesca," then kissed her. His hands became needier as they went down her back and pulled her closer to him. They wandered slowly back up and he played with her hair, touched her neck, and rested his hands on her shoulders.

His tongue was frantic in her mouth, and she returned the passion with the same intensity. But she pushed away from him. "Not here, Rudolfo. Annie's in the next room," she pleaded, out of breath.

She could see the desire in his eyes and knew it wouldn't be so easily diminished this time. "Your room?" she asked, hesitantly.

He looked into her eyes and saw indecision. He took her hands. "Francesca, I want this to be right for you. I come into your life very quickly. I travel across many lands to be with you and stay in your home with your family. I like to know the lady first before I meet her family. But . . . with you, Signorina, I already love you. We take it slow, make it right for you."

Her body wanted to go downstairs with him and make love, but logic kept her from acting on those feelings. Her mind was swimming with contradictions about what to do. Rudolfo could sense the inner struggle from the tenseness of her body.

"I go to bed, Francesca, alone. Tomorrow we get to know each other."

Tears welled up in her eyes. "I'd like that, Rudolfo. We'll start by going out for breakfast, if we can get out—I can see that it's started snowing already." She touched his hair. "Sleep well."

"Buona notte, my love." The hardest thing for him to do was to leave her and go to his room. He walked slowly down the steps and into his room. He took out his easel, pencils, and sketch paper. When everything was set up, he pulled over a chair and sat in front of the easel with his back to the door.

If he couldn't make love to Francesca, then he would do it on paper. He drew her eyes, the way he saw them before leaving her upstairs, with her dark brows. His pencil moved down and with slender strokes drew the nose. He drew the rest of her gentle face and her rounded chin. His pencil moved down farther and drew her slender shoulders, arms, and torso. He sketched her small breasts and then went back and did some shading. The pencil moved even farther down to draw her slender legs and small feet. He finished with her hair. He drew the hair he loved to look at and touch so that it fell partly in front of her left shoulder and partly down her back. When everything was drawn, he put his pencil down and stared at her.

"Rudy, you still awake?"

Rudolfo turned around and stood in front of the canvas as Annie came into the room.

"Can you tuck me in, Rudy?"

"Yes, let's go," said Rudolfo, then held out his hand. He was hoping she hadn't seen the drawing, but it was too late.

"Wait. Is that my mommy you are drawing?"

The heat rushed up Rudolfo's neck, and he said shyly, "Yes."

She went between Rudolfo and the easel, picked up his pencil, and said, "You forgot something. Mommy has a big freckle here." She drew a round mark on the left thigh. She put down the pencil, grabbed Rudolfo's hand, and said, "Let's go before Mom knows I'm up."

*   *   *

Francesca was wide awake. She tried reading and couldn't concentrate. When pacing back and forth didn't work, she decided to go see Rudolfo. When she got to his room the light was on, but he wasn't there.

She immediately recognized the person on the canvas and was shocked that he knew about her birthmark. The anger rose through her body, and as she turned to confront him she ran right into him. She pushed him away. "How dare you come into my home? I thought you cared about me—how do you know so much about me?" Her voice was choked with tears. "How do you know about my birthmark? What else do you know about me? You betrayed me."

She turned away from him. "Why are you here, Rudolfo? Tell me what you want from me," demanded Francesca.

She felt as though she would start crying if she didn't leave, but she wanted to stay to find out why he was there. She tried blinking back the tears but to no avail. "What if Annie saw the picture, did you think of that?"

He didn't move, and when she was done shouting at him he said calmly, "I not think Annie would see it."

Francesca wheeled around and faced Rudolfo. "You mean Annie did see it?"

"Please, Francesca, let me explain." When she didn't say anything, he continued. "She came down and wanted me to tuck her in. I stood in front of picture, but she see it when she came to bedroom door. She told me I forgot to draw something and then she drew in your birthmark. I sorry, Francesca. I not thinking."

Neither one moved. Rudolfo didn't want to upset her any more, so he stood there, waiting to see what she would do.

Francesca could feel the tears rolling down her face. "Rudolfo, hold me," she said, and started sobbing. He held her tight against him.

"Francesca, I so sorry," whispered Rudolfo in her ear. "Forgive me."

The crying stopped, and Rudolfo wiped away her tears. Until now he hadn't noticed that her robe was open, and he could see her red, low-cut nightgown. He tried to focus on her eyes. "It's late, Francesca. You sleep in. Annie and I make you breakfast and bring to bedroom for you."

She smiled. "With an offer like that I can't refuse."

Rudolfo laughed, "I try not to burn food."

"I won't come into the kitchen to distract you."

"If you do, don't wear red nightgown."

Feeling self-conscious, she pulled her robe closed and tied it. "Goodnight, Rudolfo, and I'm sorry, too."

Chapter Seven

"Mommy, wake up."

"Go away, Annie, let me sleep longer."

"Mom, you have to get up."

Francesca pulled the covers over her head. "Annie, please let me sleep."

Annie found an opening on the side of the bed and crawled under the covers. "Mommy," whispered Annie. She moved closer, and Francesca could smell milk on her daughter's breath. "Mommy, I made breakfast for you. Rudy helped me," said Annie, still whispering.

Francesca pulled her closer and hugged her. "Thanks, Annie."

"Rudy is holding the tray, waiting to come in. He wanted me to wake you first."

"We better get up then."

Francesca pulled down the covers slowly until just their heads were visible. She saw Rudolfo in the doorway holding a tray. "I woke her up, Rudy," Annie said.

When Annie got out of bed, Rudolfo saw Francesca's red nightgown pulled up to her thighs. She quickly put the covers back, put her pillows behind her, and sat up. He set the tray down gently on her lap, and Annie crawled back onto the bed.

Annie pointed to the plate. "These are the eggs that we fried in the pan, and we cut potatoes and fried them, too. Rudy told me to make coffee, so I stood on the stool and made coffee."

Francesca took a sip of coffee and said, "It's the best I ever tasted."

Annie sat up a little straighter and gave Rudolfo a thumbs-up.

"Did you two eat already?"

"Yep, we ate while we cooked breakfast, like Grandma does. She has to taste everything to make sure it tastes good."

"Rudolfo, sit down, you look tired," said Francesca. "Were you able to get some sleep last night?"

"I think it still jet lag."

Although it could have been jet lag, Francesca knew it was probably what happened last night that caused him not to sleep. "What should we do today? Do you two have any ideas?"

"Mommy, have you looked outside this morning? It's still snowing. I can't see across the street there is so much snow."

"I guess we stay in and read and take naps all day."

"Boring, Mom!"

Rudolfo laughed, "I got many books to read."

"Can you teach me more Italian, Rudy?"

"Yes, me teach you more Italian."

While Annie and Rudolfo watched Francesca eat, the phone rang. Annie jumped off the bed and was off to the kitchen to answer the phone.

"Francesca, you sleep well?"

"Yes, I did. I'm so sorry about last night. The picture you drew took me by surprise. Then the anger came so fast I couldn't control it."

"I already forgive you."

"You're so good to me, Rudolfo. I wish we had some time alone today. With the weather like it is, I don't think that will happen."

"Don't worry Francesca, we make time together. We can make something warm and talk after Annie goes to bed tonight."

"I would like that."

Annie ran back into the room. "Mommy, Grandma can't get her car out of the driveway. She wanted to come over again, but now she won't be able to."

"Maybe by the end of the day the plows will have gone through and we can get out," said Francesca.

"We should go to Grandma's house so Rudy can see where she lives. It's a cool house, Rudy. She has an attic that I like to play in and you can come and play up there with me."

"Attic?"

"In one of her bedrooms she has a ladder in the closet and we can go up the ladder and look through all her stuff." Annie looked at her mom. "Can Rudy come up there with me?"

"Only if he wants to."

"I go with you," Rudolfo said. "You show me all your grandma's things."

"I'm going to go call her back and tell her if we get plowed out we will come to her house." With that said, Annie ran back into the kitchen.

"She has lots of energy for one so little," said Rudolfo.

"She sure does. Why don't I help you with the dishes?"

Rudolfo took the tray and went to the kitchen while Francesca got dressed. On the way out of the bedroom, she stopped and pulled on her wool socks.

*　　*　　*

"Mommy, Grandma says we can come over whenever the plows go through. I'm going to get dressed and then can I go outside and play in the snow?"

"Make sure you dress warm."

"Rudy, will you come outside with me?" asked Annie.

58

"No, no, me not go outside. Too much snow, and it cold outside."

"It can't be too cold, Rudy, the sun is shining," said Annie, as she went to get dressed.

"Why don't you come outside, Rudolfo? We can help Annie build a snowman. Have you ever done that before? It's something you can brag about to Filipo."

"Ah, Filipo, I told him I would do something on computer when I got here. I told him I don't know computers but he thought you would have one."

"I do, in my office. Do you have his e-mail address?"

"It's in my wallet."

"I'll go tell Annie where we are and I'll meet you downstairs."

*   *   *

Francesca turned on the computer. "Sit here, Rudolfo, and you can learn all about computers."

"No, no, you do it for me."

"No, no, you learn how to do it and then you can turn on the computer and e-mail Filipo anytime you want."

She showed him how to connect to the Internet and to get into her e-mail. He took the napkin out of his wallet and typed in the address where Francesca indicated.

He wrote down Francesca's password and e-mail address so he could get in again. She pointed to where he could type his message.

"I don't type well."

"Do you do all your writing with pen and paper?"

"Yes."

Francesca told him what to do when he was done typing and then left him alone to write to Filipo. She went upstairs to check on Annie, who was already outside. Francesca opened the window. "Annie, is it cold out there?"

"It's warm, Mommy. Come outside with me."

"I'll be out as soon as I find my boots."

"Mommy, make sure you bring Rudy with you."

"I'll try, honey," said Francesca, and she closed the window.

Francesca went to the front closet and found her snow boots and put on her winter jacket, stocking hat, and leather gloves. She was about to go downstairs to see if Rudolfo would go outside with her when he appeared at the top of the steps wearing his coat, gloves, boots and scarf. "Are you going outside, or are you just cold?" asked Francesca with a smile.

"I go outside and play in snow. Do we have more tea? When I come in I be cold and need to warm up."

"Come here, Rudolfo. I'll warm you up."

He came to her and she put her arms around him. It wasn't easy with the bulk of their winter attire. "I kiss you, no?" asked Francesca.

"You tease. You kiss me, yes!"

She kissed him. "I like your kisses, Rudolfo. We better get outside before Annie comes in to see what we're doing."

He kissed her again. "Now we go."

She pulled on her boots and they went outside.

As soon as Francesca stepped off the back steps, a snowball was headed in her direction. She ducked just in time, and it hit Rudolfo in the shoulder. "Rudolfo, you have to be alert out here with Annie. She likes to throw snowballs. Let's throw some back at her."

"Okay, Annie, look out!" yelled Francesca. They threw the snowballs, but missed as Annie dove to the ground.

"You guys missed me."

They tried again, but Annie was too quick for them. They decided to make a snowman, and Annie told Rudolfo what to do. "You start rolling this snowball until it gets to be a big snowball, so we can put three big snowballs on top of each other." Annie handed Rudolfo the snowball. "And you're not allowed to throw this one."

"Okay, me not throw at you. Can I throw at your mother?"

"Yes! Hurry before she looks up at us." Rudolfo hurled the snowball and it landed in the middle of Francesca's back.

"Hey, who did that?"

She turned around and threw a snowball back at Rudolfo, but she missed. "Let's make the snowman now, Rudy," said Annie.

He made his own snowball and started rolling it in the snow. It took most of the afternoon to finish the snowman because they stopped at times to make snow angels and to shovel some of the driveway. Rudolfo helped Annie put on the finishing touches, with a carrot nose and rocks from Annie's room for the eyes and mouth. They decided that the plows would not be coming today and went inside. Annie called Grandma, and Francesca made supper out of the leftovers from their dinner the day before.

Rudolfo went to put on some dry clothes. When he returned, he made hot tea. "I'm still cold, Francesca. Do you ever warm up in winter months?"

"Yes, we wear winter underwear and wool socks all year," said Francesca with a laugh.

"You go put on something warm. I finish dinner."

"I'll go check on Annie, too."

"Remember, we spend tonight together and talk."

"I remember, Rudolfo. I'm looking forward to it."

*   *   *

Annie kept the conversation going most of the evening while they talked about the snow, about what they would do tomorrow if it kept up, and about how the plows had not yet arrived. "We'll have to make more snowmen, Rudy. Grandma's attic will have to wait. Mommy, why aren't the plows here yet?"

"Since it keeps snowing, once they plow the main roads they have to turn around and do it again. I'm sure they'll get to it by next week."

"Next week!"

"Mommy's joking, Rudy. Aren't you, Mommy?"

"I'm joking. Why don't you call Grandma and then go to bed? Please tell Grandma I want to talk to her."

"Do I have to go to bed?"

"I read you story," offered Rudolfo.

"Rudolfo wants to ask you about Christmas, too," Francesca said.

"Are you staying for Christmas?"

"No, I be in New York with my sister. She wants to know if you come to New York with your mommy and grandma."

Annie ran to her mom. "Can we go to New York, Mommy? Can I fly on an airplane?"

"Rudolfo has nieces and nephews that you'll be able to play with in New York." She looked at Annie. "Do you really want to go?"

"Yes, can we go, Mommy?"

"It will be a special Christmas with Rudolfo's family. Let's call Grandma and ask her if she wants to go."

*   *   *

Francesca was still on the phone when Rudolfo finished reading Annie a story and entered the kitchen. He went behind her and put his arms around her waist. "Francesca. You talk to me now, yes?"

"I'll call you tomorrow, Mom. Goodnight." Francesca hung up the phone and turned in Rudolfo's arms. "Mom wants to go with us. She says she has a friend in New York that she hasn't seen in a long time and would love to see again. She'll call him first to see if he has plans."

"I glad you come to New York. I call Carmella tomorrow and tell her."

"Can you e-mail her?"

"She give me her address. You have to tell me again how to e-mail."

"Let's go down and use the computer."

Chapter Eight

Rudolfo sat at the computer, read from his notes, and was able to bring up Francesca's e-mail account. Francesca stood behind him with her hands on his shoulders, amazed at how well he was doing. "You e-mail like you've always been doing it, Rudolfo."

"You good teacher, Francesca. I see Filipo's name. He write back to me?"

"Yes," said Francesca, pleased that his friend had written back to him already.

"How do I read it?"

"Just click on it. Then you click on "Reply" and answer him back. You are doing very well for not ever using a computer. Are you sure you never did this before?"

"I sure. I take good notes."

"When you are done, we can sit down here by the fireplace. I'll start a fire and you can make the hot chocolate."

"Me hurry, Francesca."

*   *   *

They were sitting on the couch, and Rudolfo commented on the nice fire.

"The hot chocolate is good, too, Rudolfo."

"How you make fire so fast?"

"See that switch on the wall? I moved it up and the fire started."

Rudolfo let out a deep, hardy laugh. Francesca had never heard him laugh like that before. "I thought you go outside in snow and bring in logs to start fire." He laughed again. "You just move switch."

"Glad you find that so amusing."

"You sit closer, Francesca. I'm getting cold, fire fading. Unless you move switch again," said Rudolfo, and he started laughing all over again.

She set her hot chocolate on the coffee table and put her head on his shoulder. "I'm starting to feel more comfortable with you, Rudolfo. You don't seem like a stranger anymore. Annie likes you, and that means so much to me. She was doing all right with me and her grandmother, but I believe she likes having a man around. I do, too."

"I like Annie. She good kid." He set his hot chocolate down and took one of her feet, slid off her wool sock, and started massaging her foot.

She got comfortable. "Oh, Rudolfo, that feels wonderful."

"I keep doing it, no?"

"You keep doing it, yes!"

He massaged her foot and then moved up to her calf and then to her knee. He started up to her thigh. "Rudolfo," whispered Francesca. "I thought we were going to talk and get to know each other first."

"Talk to me Francesca, and I keep doing what I'm doing."

"I can't concentrate if you keep doing that."

"If you can't talk, then I keep doing this."

He kept massaging her leg and wouldn't look up at her. He pulled off her other wool sock and started massaging that foot. "I think you need to make me some more hot chocolate, Rudolfo."

"I make when I done with your foot."

"I think you should stop and make it now."

"If you getting cold, move switch on fireplace," offered Rudolfo, without laughing and without looking up.

His body shifted on the couch, and he moved his hands up her legs and rested them on her thighs. He wanted to keep going but he wanted to find out if she was ready first, ready for him. Would she be afraid and want to wait? When they were alone together, Rudolfo could only think of touching her and nothing else.

He looked up at her and focused on her eyes. The flickering of the fire was casting shadows against the wall. She was calm, he noticed, and the look of indecision was absent from her blue eyes. "Francesca, are you still afraid?"

"No, Rudolfo, not anymore."

He touched her face, moved over and kissed her, a deep kiss that expressed his love for her. She held his hands while he kissed her more deeply, more sensuously. The thought of Annie seeing them crossed their minds at the same time, and they broke away from each other.

"It feels so right to be here with you. I don't know why, it just does." She put her head on his shoulder and wrapped her arms around his. "Tell me about when you were sick."

"I was packing and I was so out of breath that I had to sit down. I start to get chilled and crawled in bed to warm up, but nothing I do make me any warmer. I call Filipo, and that's the last I remember until I wake up in hospital, with my good friend beside me." He took a sip of his hot chocolate. "The fever break and then I get migraine. Doctor give me medicine for headache and send me home. I fine now. Doctor tell me not to travel. But I have to see you."

"I would've understood if you had postponed your trip a little longer." She took his hand. "If you ever feel sick at all, you let me know. I don't want anything to happen to you."

"I will. I promise."

The room was warm. Rudolfo pulled Francesca closer to him, and they shut their eyes and enjoyed being close to each other. As much as he wanted to make love to her, he decided this was best.

*　　*　　*

Francesca woke up and expected Rudolfo to be next to her. She sat up, pulled off the afghan, and headed up the stairs. She could smell bacon and eggs and a hint of coffee.

Annie and Rudolfo were eating breakfast together. "Mommy, Rudy told me you were downstairs sleeping on the couch. Are you hungry?"

"I'm starving. I'll get a plate and join you."

She poured a cup of coffee and loaded her plate with eggs and bacon. She was hungrier than she had thought. "Rudy, why do you keep smiling at my mom?"

Embarrassed, Rudolfo answered, "She got funny hair."

Francesca started laughing. She had never thought to comb her hair or see what she looked like. "I'll have to shower and comb my hair after breakfast."

"Grandma called. The plows went through and she wants us to come over later. I told her you would call her back. Rudy said he was coming, too."

Francesca smiled at Rudolfo and said, "I'm glad."

*　　*　　*

"It's so good to see you again, Rudolfo. How do you like Minnesota after the snowstorm?" asked Rose.

She took his coat and he replied, "I still like Minnesota. Three nice ladies live here."

"Grandma, can me and Rudy go up in your attic?"

"May Rudy and I go to the attic?" corrected Francesca.

"Grandma, can we?"

Rose laughed. "Yes, you may go, but maybe Rudolfo wants to have some tea first."

"We go to attic. I have tea later," said Rudolfo.

Annie walked past Rudolfo and said, "It's this way. Follow me."

Rudolfo winked at Francesca, "You come get me if I up there too long."

"I will," said Francesca.

He followed Annie to the far bedroom. Rose poured Francesca coffee and they sat at the table. "He really is enjoying his stay, isn't he?"

"Yes, and Annie likes him so much. They made me breakfast in bed the day after our big dinner, and this morning they had breakfast all made by the time I got up. I'll put on weight if I keep eating so much."

"Good, you're too thin. A little extra weight will do you good."

"You're right."

"I know I'm right. You're way too thin."

"Mom, I think I love him. He's so kind and never gets angry."

"I know you do."

"How do you know?"

"I can see it on your face. You've never looked so happy."

"I am happy. At times I'm still a little apprehensive about our relationship, but overall he makes me happy."

Rose thought for a minute and then said, "I can't think of anything to be apprehensive about. He makes great pies, he's good with Annie, and he is pleasant to me."

"You're probably right, Mom. It just confuses me at times how we met."

"Mommy! Grandma!" Annie called. "Rudy is sick and he can't come down the ladder. Hurry Mom! He needs help!"

Francesca flew out of her chair, ran down the hall, and hurried up the ladder. Rose followed. Rudolfo was sitting in the middle of the attic with his head in his hands. She went over to him, knelt down, and touched his leg. "Rudolfo, what's the matter?"

He looked up and was so pale that Francesca worried he would pass out. "I not like being up so high." He attempted a smile but his lips were trembling.

"Can I help you down?"

"In a couple minutes I be ready." He took her hand and held it tight. "I hope I not scare Annie."

Rose and Annie were sitting on an antique trunk that had belonged to Rose's grandmother. It was filled with antique jewelry, shoes, old clothes, and a wedding dress—the dress Rose had worn at her wedding.

Annie and Rudolfo had been kneeling in front of the trunk when Rudolfo looked across the room and out a small window. It was then that he realized how high up he was, and the room closed in on him and he started to get dizzy.

He had felt queasy climbing the ladder but ignored the feeling because he knew Annie wanted to show him all the treasures in the attic. Then the queasiness had caught up with him and he had needed to sit down.

Rose had her arm around Annie as they watched Francesca and Rudolfo. Annie pulled on Rose's shirt and whispered in her grandma's ear. "Is Rudy going to be okay, Grandma?"

Rose noticed tears on Annie's face. "Yes, honey, he'll be okay."

"You promise?"

"I promise," said Rose firmly.

Rose held her tight. "I think he's afraid of being up so high in such a closed space. Some people are like that. As soon as your mommy gets him downstairs he will be fine, Annie."

"I don't want him to be sick again and go away. I want him to stay and be my daddy."

Now Rose had tears in her eyes.

Francesca helped Rudolfo up. "I stay here a minute, Francesca."

After a couple of minutes they turned around, and when he looked at Annie she ran over to him and put her arms around his legs. He patted her head. "I be okay, Annie. When your mom get me downstairs, you make me some tea."

When she looked up at him through her tears, he felt terrible for putting her through this. "Take my hand, Annie, you help me, too." She wiped away the tears with her shirt sleeve and took his hand.

"Follow me, Rudy. I'll help you get to the ladder."

Once Rudolfo was down the ladder and had his feet on the floor, the dizziness quickly passed. He worried that he had put Annie and Francesca through unnecessary grief, since the feeling of nausea had lifted so quickly, and he wondered if he had overreacted. Then he realized that no, the dizziness was real. Now that his feet were safely on the floor, he felt much better.

Francesca walked with him over to the couch and they sat down. Annie went straight to the kitchen with Rose following her and started making tea.

"You scared me, Rudolfo," said Francesca. "You looked so pale and so sick. I'm glad you are better now." Francesca put her head on his shoulder. "I couldn't bear to lose you."

He stroked her hair and turned her face to his, "You won't lose me, Francesca."

*   *   *

"Hurry, Grandma, bring the tray, the tea is ready. Rudy needs tea so he can feel better."

Rose had been quiet while Annie took charge of the kitchen and ordered her around. "Grandma, get the water in the kettle, and find the tray you use for parties. Do you have any biscuits? Rudy likes biscuits."

After Annie's comment about her wanting Rudolfo to be her daddy, Rose could understand why she wanted Rudolfo to feel better as soon as possible.

"Grandma, you carry the tray. Everything is already on it. I'll meet you in the living room." Annie raced out of the kitchen.

She saw Rudolfo with his arm around her mother and talking as Francesca rested her head on his shoulder. Annie sat next to him and moved his other arm and put it around her shoulders. "Grandma is coming with the tea. Are you feeling better, Rudy?" She looked up at him. "You look better. We'll play down here, okay, Rudy? There's just dumb stuff in the attic anyway."

"Annie, would you do me a favor?" asked Rudolfo, knowing she loved the things in the trunk.

Annie jumped off the couch and almost collided with Rose and the tray of tea and cookies. "What do you want, Rudy? Do you need me to bring you anything?"

"I'm fine, Annie. The dress and hat you show me in big trunk—you get it and try it on for me. I like to see it."

"You would?!"

"I can't go up, but ask your mom if you can bring them down."

Annie's worried face turned into a big smile. "You want me to wear the shoes, too?"

"Yes." Rudolfo laughed at the thought of the big high-heeled shoes on Annie's little feet.

Annie went over and took a cup of tea off the tray, very carefully handing it to Rudolfo. "You drink your tea and I'll be right back."

"There's a bag next to the trunk, Annie. Put the clothes in there. They will be easier to carry," instructed Rose.

Annie went off with a purpose and a smile on her face. Rose said, "Annie was so worried about you, Rudolfo, that I'm glad she's in a better mood now. Thank you for asking her to try on the clothes. That's her favorite thing to do."

"She so excited showing me treasures, and then I start to feel sick."

"How are you really feeling?" asked Rose.

"I fine. As soon as my feet touch floor, I feel good again."

They looked up when they heard the trunk slam shut. "She must have all her treasures in the bag," said Francesca. "She'll want me to help her get dressed." She hated to leave the warmth of Rudolfo's body against hers. She wanted to be alone with him again. Maybe tonight after Annie went to bed they could spend some more time together.

Francesca went off to the guest room to meet Annie, and Rose went over and sat next to Rudolfo. "Annie likes you."

"I like her, too."

"She told me she wants you to be her daddy."

"I like to be her daddy."

"What happens when you go back to Florence?"

Rudolfo could sense her concern and chose his words carefully. "I ask Francesca to marry me, then I be Annie's daddy."

"Will you stay in Minnesota, or ask them to move to Florence with you? Personally I don't want them to move away from me. We're too close a family to be separated."

"We go to New York, I ask Francesca to marry me, and I go back to Florence. Annie and Francesca can come to Florence on spring break, then we all come back and I live in Minnesota."

"You love Florence. Can you leave so easily?"

"In the past, a woman wanted me to move away from Florence and I wouldn't do it, and Carmella always want me to move to America. I love Francesca and I move anywhere she wants me to."

"What if Francesca says no?"

"I hope she say yes. I never thought what I would do if she say no."

"I hope she says yes, too."

"I love Francesca very much."

"I know you do. Francesca has never been lucky in the love department, but I can sense that you do love her and would do anything for her."

"She love me too, no?"

Rose laughed. "She loves you, too, yes."

Rudolfo took a sip of his now cool tea, and Rose continued. "Francesca tells me you're an artist and author and that you have books published."

"I lucky. Publishers like what I write."

"You're very talented, and I don't think it was luck at all. How old are you, Rudolfo?" asked Rose, for no apparent reason.

"I thought in America you not ask someone their age."

"That's only for ladies, not men," said Rose with a smile on her face.

"Here we come, Grandma and Rudy!" yelled Annie from the hallway.

"You're off the hook this time, Rudolfo," said Rose.

Annie came around the corner with a dusty-rose Victorian dress on and matching high-heeled shoes. Her curly hair was tucked under a large hat with dried flowers around the brim. She was holding tightly to her mother's hand as she shuffled the shoes forward. Francesca had applied some rouge to Annie's cheeks and dusted her face with powder.

Rudolfo stood and bowed. "You look so lovely in your beautiful clothes that we should go dancing."

Annie laughed. "Can we really go dancing?"

"You put music on, we dance."

Annie looked at Rose. "Grandma, do you have any music we can dance to?"

"I pick you up, we can dance better that way."

Rose went over to the CD player, pushed "Play," and a waltz started.

When he picked her up her shoes fell off, but she didn't notice. While they were dancing her hat kept hitting Rudolfo in the forehead, so she took it off and tossed it to her mother.

"Francesca, what will you and Annie do when Rudolfo goes back to Florence?" Rose wanted to know if she was thinking marriage. If she sent him back to Florence with a no, she didn't think Annie would recover.

"I'm trying not to think about it."

Rudolfo and Annie waltzed by, both smiling and having a good time as they danced.

"Well, you should think about it. You also need to talk to Annie about how she's feeling."

Francesca heard Rudolfo and Annie laughing and knew her mother was right. She needed to have a heart-to-heart talk with Annie, and she already knew the outcome. Annie would want Rudolfo to stay.

*   *   *

The days passed quickly before Christmas. Francesca and Rudolfo weren't able to be alone again, as Annie clung to Rudolfo as much as she could. It was very busy this time of year for the leather company Francesca worked for, and she was attending meetings and working long hours at the office. When she did have some free time, she would go out shopping for Christmas presents. Rudolfo gave her Carmella's address, and whenever she bought a present for his nieces and nephews she would mail it off to New York.

When she got home at night she was exhausted. Two days before they were to travel to New York was the day of the company holiday party at Jax Café in NE Minneapolis. She asked Rudolfo to go with her and he happily accepted.

Chapter Nine

Francesca wore the black dress she had bought while shopping with her mother on the day Rudolfo was supposed to arrive in Minnesota. It took her almost two hours to get dressed. She wanted everything to be perfect. Rose was already at the house, ready to take care of Annie, and told Francesca she would sleep there overnight so that they could stay out as late as they wanted.

Rudolfo was in the living room with Annie next to him. Playing cards were spread out on the coffee table, and Annie was showing him how to play solitaire. Rudolfo had on a black suit, white shirt, and green tie. His hair was pulled back and tied with a leather strap. He looked exceptionally handsome all dressed up. When Rose came over, she was surprised at how much the suit changed his appearance. She was used to him in his brown trousers, tan shirt, and green tweed jacket.

Francesca came into the living room, and Rudolfo looked up and let out a sigh, then stood. "Francesca," he whispered. "Ah, my lady, your beauty excites me. I'm a lucky man to be with you this evening."

Her hair was swept up and held with gold clips in the back, which Rudolfo thought made the soft features in her face more prominent. He definitely noticed how her dress clung to her slim body. Tightness welled in his whole being and he wanted her.

Annie kept playing. Rose was in the kitchen making supper, and Rudolfo was still staring at Francesca. She noticed how handsome he looked and she felt weak. Annie looked around Rudolfo and at her mother. "Mommy, you look nice," she said. "Can I go to the party with you and Rudy?"

No longer mesmerized by Rudolfo's presence, Francesca came over to her daughter, but first Rudolfo took Francesca in his arms, kissed her, and whispered in her ear, "I love you."

"I love you, too."

"Can I come, Mom?"

Francesca sat down by Annie. Rudolfo noticed how her dress moved up to her thighs. He turned around quickly and joined Rose in the kitchen.

"No, Annie, Rudolfo and I are going alone. Grandma is going to help you pack tonight for our trip to New York."

"Okay," said Annie, and she went back to the cards.

That was too easy, thought Francesca. She took her long black wool coat from the closet. Before she went into the kitchen, she looked at Annie, who had a big smile on her face.

"Would you like to drive, Rudolfo?" asked Francesca.

"No, no, no, I don't drive. I drive bicycle, but you dressed too nice to get on back of bicycle."

Rose laughed. "I guess you'll be driving, Francesca. You look beautiful, honey. Go and have a good time and don't worry about getting home early."

"Thanks, Mom," said Francesca, hugging her good-bye.

Rudolfo did the same, taking Rose off guard. He's a strong man, she thought. There wasn't anything she could find that was wrong with Rudolfo, and sometimes that worried her.

"I take care of Francesca and make sure she drive safely," Rudolfo said.

"Have a good time. Goodnight."

*   *   *

"Rudolfo, would you like to see a parade?"

"We go to party. They have parade at party?"

"No. They have happy hour in a half hour." Francesca thought she'd better explain what happy hour was. "They serve drinks and food before dinner. It's a time to socialize and introduce spouses and significant others to coworkers and bosses. We don't really need to get in on that if you want to see a parade first."

"I want to see parade first. Where is it?"

"It's in downtown Minneapolis and it's called the Hollidazzle Parade. It's their annual parade during the holidays. The people, the floats, everything has lights on it."

"I want to see parade," said Rudolfo, excited about seeing all the lights and a parade at the same time.

Francesca pulled into the Orchestra Hall parking ramp on Eleventh Avenue and parked the car. They took the elevator down to ground level and walked across the street, joining others already waiting along the curb on the Nicollet Mall.

There were small children with their empty bags all ready for candy, waiting for the parade to start. Rudolfo stood behind Francesca with his arms around her and watched the people along the parade route.

"You cold, Francesca?"

"Just a little chilled. Whenever I've come before, it's been freezing. Luckily it's forty degrees out and no wind." She snuggled closer to his warm body. "Here comes the police car. That means the parade is starting."

"Look, Francesca, the children have stars on their necks and all lit up."

She looked back at him, and he was smiling like a child himself. "Do you like the parade so far?"

"Yes, I like. Look, the float with the Wizard of Oz. Carmella has video, we watch all the time. Can we stay here and not go to party?" asked Rudolfo in a joking voice.

"We have to go to the party after the parade is over."

Francesca didn't know how it happened, but Rudolfo was standing on the curb and she was behind him. He put his hand out and the Mother Goose character gave him a high five. Several more floats passed and he was helping the children standing next to him catch the candy and put it in their bags. He was enjoying the parade so much and it was over all too quickly, and when he saw the police car again, he turned to her with a sad look on his face. "Why police car back?"

"The police go by when it's the end of the parade. It's time to go to the party."

"Are you sure there's not more?"

"I'm sure, Rudolfo." She took his hand and led him to the corner where they crossed to get to their car. "The party will be just as much fun, without the lights."

"Party going to be spectacular?"

Francesca laughed. "We can go see the parade again tomorrow night, if you want."

"Yes, yes. Annie come too?"

"She would love to come. Mom will want to come, too. Are you up to being outnumbered again?"

"I love being with lovely ladies, especially the three of you."

*　　*　　*

They found the room at Jax where the party was already under way. The room was filled with smells of good food, and sounds of holiday cheer. The round tables looked elegant with white tablecloths and lit candles. The bartender was serving drinks at the mirrored bar. People were mingling and eating hors d'oeuvres.　　"This is my friend, Rudolfo Vittori. Rudolfo, this is my manager, Mike Gerard."

They shook hands. "I met Francesca in Florence. Have you been there?" asked Rudolfo.

"No, I let Francesca do all the traveling. I will have to get there some day."

"Yes, after you see Florence you'll keep coming back."

"You certainly would be an authority, and of course Francesca talks about it for days when she gets back from Italy."

"You let me know when you are coming, and you can stay with me."

"I'll hold you to that."

Francesca hadn't thought Rudolfo would be staying long in America, but to extend an invitation like that seemed to confirm that he would never come back to America. Rudolfo saw the sad look on her face and took her hand. He added, "Let me know when you come. I might be here in America."

Mike touched Rudolfo's shoulder, "Why don't you two sit at my table? We'll all sit together from our office."

They sat with Mike and his wife, Jan. Rudolfo talked easily with the others at the table, and Francesca was glad he fit in so well. Jan and Rudolfo got into a discussion of women working, and with a grin on his face, Rudolfo said that a woman should be at home, making tea and biscuits for the man in her life.

When they were finished eating, the guest speaker went up front and spoke about resolutions for the New Year. He suggested steps to raise sales and how to keep the customer as the number-one priority. Rudolfo took in the message, but instead of sales thought of his number-one priority in life, Francesca.

The speaker, in conclusion, tied all the points together about salesmanship and wished everyone a happy holiday.

Francesca was enjoying the speaker as well and looked over at Rudolfo periodically. Judging from the intensity with which he was listening, Francesca didn't think he would notice her taking his hand, but she was wrong. When she touched his hand he squeezed it and pulled it into his lap, all the while looking straight ahead.

After everyone stopped clapping, people stood up and started saying good-bye.

"Francesca, have a safe trip to New York, and get in touch with me when you get back," Mike said.

"I will, Mike. Thank you."

"Rudolfo, it was a pleasure to meet you."

"I enjoyed meeting you, too."

Jan extended her hand to Rudolfo, and he took it. "I'm going to keep working, Rudolfo. Mike can make his own biscuits," Jan said.

They both laughed. "Mike is still a lucky man. Have a Merry Christmas," he said, then kissed her hand.

Not sure how to interpret the smile on his wife's face, Mike put his arm around her and led her to the coat room.

"Let's go to the parade again," said Rudolfo.

"The parade is over."

"I don't want to go home. I want to spend time with you alone."

The word "home" echoed through Francesca's mind. It did feel like he belonged in her home. He was so good with Annie and he was always home to talk to, and he made her biscuits. Yes, home, that was where they belonged together.

"Where do you want to go?" Francesca said.

"Let's go to the bar and have some wine," Rudolfo suggested.

"Okay, we'll pick up our coats when we're done, but first I have to go to the rest room."

Instead of waiting for her, Rudolfo went directly to the bar. He found the bartender and talked to him, then handed him something. The bartender nodded his head, and Rudolfo went out into the hall to find Francesca waiting.

"I thought you had left and gone to the parade."

Rudolfo laughed. "I go nowhere without my lovely signorina."

They sat at a corner booth, and the bartender came right over to take their drink orders. "White wine for me," said Rudolfo.

"I'll have red," Francesca said.

The bartender said, "The white wine is especially good this evening. Why don't you try some?"

"No, thank you. I like the red wine better."

The bartender left, and Francesca said, "I wonder why the waitress didn't take our order."

"He sees lovely lady and can't help himself."

They drank their wine and talked about their evening. When their glasses were empty, the bartender cleared them away and replaced them with two glasses of white wine. By the time Francesca noticed, he was already back behind the bar.

"You don't like white wine?"

"I don't mind it," she said, and took a sip.

They talked about the upcoming trip to New York and about how excited Annie was about traveling. They took their time drinking the second glass of wine, knowing that Rose was taking care of Annie and sleeping over.

"I noticed your English is getting better."

"Annie is giving me lessons while I give her lessons in Italian."

"I felt guilty leaving you two home alone all the time, but it looks like you put the time to good use." She looked at her wine glass and held it up. "Rudolfo!"

"Yes, my love," he said with a grin on his face.

"There's a ring at the bottom of my glass!" She drank the rest of the wine and took out the ring. She held it up. "It's beautiful, Rudolfo."

"Marry me, Francesca. Will you marry me?"

Chapter Ten

Tears were streaming down her face. If I say yes, he has to stay. She went over to him and sat in his lap. "Yes, Rudolfo, I'll marry you."

He kissed her lips and then he was kissing away the tears. "Francesca, I love you. I make you happy."

"I know you will." She put her arms around him. It felt right in his arms, and now she could be there whenever she wanted. She kissed him. "I love you, Rudolfo."

The patrons started clapping. Francesca felt the heat rising in her face.

"You better sit down, everyone is watching us," said Rudolfo in a gentle voice. Francesca looked around, and people were raising their glasses and nodding at them. She went to her own side of the booth and noticed that the bartender must have brought a bottle of champagne to their table. Rudolfo poured the champagne and made a toast.

"To the love of my life." He raised his glass. "May we always be good parents to Annie, and be good to each other."

She sipped her champagne. Annie loves him too, and now he will be a part of her life.

"I adopt Annie, no?"

Francesca smiled at him. "If all these people weren't around, I'd be back in your lap. You adopt, Annie, yes!"

He took her left hand and put the ring on her finger. "You like ring?"

"I love the ring." She looked at it more closely this time. There was a small diamond in the middle with emerald chips encircling it. "How did you know I liked green stones?"

"One day when you were out shopping and going to meetings, I called a cab. Annie and I went shopping. She looked over all the rings, and when she saw this one she knew you would like it."

"Annie knew you were going to ask me to marry you? And she picked out the ring?"

"Yes. She worked hard at not telling my secret."

"I'm sure she did, since she can't keep quiet about anything. Hey, is that why, when I left her tonight, she was smiling?"

"She was almost bursting with not telling you. She didn't tell her grandmother either."

"Then we should go home so Annie and Mom can go to bed." Francesca looked down at the ring. "I'm sure they haven't slept at all yet."

"Let's finish our champagne first, then we go home." He took her hand. "Why don't you come and sit next to me?" He started to laugh. "But not in my lap. We save that for later."

*   *   *

As Francesca put the key in the door, she turned to Rudolfo. "Do you think they're awake?"

"Annie might be sleeping, but as soon as we walk in the house she'll wake up." And that's exactly what she did. They went through the front door and Annie was waiting for them.

"Mommy, Mommy, did you have fun?" She wiped the sleep out of her eyes.

Francesca kept her left hand in her pocket, and Annie kept looking at it. "Are you cold, Mom?"

"No, it's quite warm in here. Did you and Grandma make a fire?"

They all looked up when Rose answered. "We kept very busy. Annie would not sit still. She even suggested we go to the party and surprise you."

Rudolfo winked at Annie, then put his arm around Francesca. "We have an announcement to make."

Francesca took her hand out of her pocket and held it up. "Rudolfo asked me to marry him."

Rose went to her daughter and embraced her, then took her hand and looked at the ring. "The ring is beautiful." She stepped back and looked at it some more. "I'm so happy for you both."

"Did you say yes, Mommy?" asked Annie. She went to Rudolfo, "Did she say yes, Rudy?"

Francesca picked up her daughter. "I heard you picked out the ring. You did a great job, Annie."

"Wait a minute," said Rose. "Annie picked out the ring?"

Francesca put Annie down, and Rudolfo and Annie did a high five. "Our plan worked," said Annie, pleased.

"Okay, somebody needs to fill me in," said Rose.

After Annie gave her grandmother every detail, she said, "Does anyone want tea or coffee?"

"It's late, Annie, I think we should all go to bed," said Rose.

Rudolfo looked at Annie's sad face. "I would like some tea, do you need some help?" She took his hand and led him to the kitchen.

Rose and Francesca sat on the sofa. "It's a beautiful ring, Francesca."

"Yes, it is. It makes me happy that Annie was in on the secret, which tells me she approves."

"She approves all right," said Rose. Unlike the gas fireplace downstairs, Rose stoked the fire. "She talked about him all night. He's the new president of her playhouse now. He was voted in unanimously." Rose stood, continuing to look at the fire. After several minutes, she turned. "She loves him, and he loves her. It makes me so happy that you are getting married."

"It makes me happy, too, Mom. Annie needs a father, and I need him, too." She thought back to the lost years without true love, and how one day in a small café on the other side of the world she met the love of her life. "Mom," she said, "we haven't talked about where we will live. It would be nice if we could keep both places and travel back and forth."

"It's something you'll have to think about. Just remember that you can't be taking Annie out of school all the time."

Chapter Eleven

They were leaving for New York tomorrow, and Annie and Rudolfo wanted their last night before traveling to be a special one. As Annie shared with Rudolfo, "A celebration of Mom getting married, me flying on a plane, and Grandma coming with us." They took a cab to the grocery store and bought steak, fresh vegetables, and cake for dessert.

Rudolfo noticed that a woman was following them as they went up and down the aisles. He didn't think much of it until he observed her in the cereal aisle. She was holding a cereal box in front of her as though reading the label, but instead of doing that she was looking straight at Annie. He noticed her doing the same thing several more times when Annie wanted to stop to look at something.

Rudolfo, for some reason that he wasn't sure of, wanted Annie out of the store as soon as possible. He paid for their purchases, picked her up in his arms along with the bag of groceries, and called a cab on the cell phone Francesca had given him. The woman stopped and looked at magazines while they waited for the cab.

It was more than ten minutes, and the cab hadn't arrived yet. Rudolfo was getting very anxious. He had read about child kidnappings, and he wanted to get Annie home as soon as possible. He would never forgive himself if something happened to her.

Annie was talking about the celebration they had planned for tonight, but Rudolfo couldn't concentrate on what she was saying. He had only one thing on his mind—Annie's safety.

Letting out a sigh when the cab pulled up, he walked out with Annie still in his arms. He glanced back, and the woman was looking up from her magazine at Annie. Once outside, Rudolfo told the cab driver the address and asked him to hurry. He sat in back with Annie next to him. The groceries were in the front seat with the driver.

When the cab arrived at Francesca's home, Rudolfo paid, grabbed Annie's hand, and maneuvered the groceries out of the front seat. There was a car a half a block away, and from what he could see, the driver looked like the woman in the store.

Rudolfo didn't let go of Annie's hand as he took out the house key, went to the door and opened it. He picked up the groceries he had set on the ground and went into the house. The car was still there. He shut the door and bolted the lock.

"Rudy, what's the matter?"

"I'm just thinking about tonight, and then traveling tomorrow." Changing the subject, he said, "Are you packed?"

"I don't know what to pack. Can you help me? Grandma and I didn't do any packing while you were at your party with mom."

First they planned the evening, and then they helped each other pack. Annie called Rose while Rudolfo started dinner, to tell her what time to come over and to plan on staying the night. Annie wanted to play outside, but Rudolfo told her no. He'd looked down the block and the car was still there. He wasn't sure how to call the police in America, and to ask Annie to help him would only scare her.

He felt relieved seconds later when Francesca drove up. When she got out of her car, he noticed that the woman drove off.

"How are my two favorite people?" asked Francesca when she came in.

"Mommy, we started dinner."

"It sure smells good." She took off her coat and hung it up. When she returned to the kitchen, she asked, "Who wants to go to the parade tonight?"

Rudolfo said no immediately. He was thinking of the woman who had been following them and didn't want to go outside, especially in the dark with a crowd of people.

"I thought you wanted to go again," said Francesca, feeling disappointed.

Sensing her mood change, he went over to her. "I don't want to be selfish and go to a parade when we have so much to do before we travel tomorrow." He stroked her hair. "Besides, you look tired."

"If Rudy doesn't want to go, I don't either," said Annie.

Francesca put her arms around him. "Thank you, I am tired. I'll go change and start packing. Let me know if you need any help with dinner."

He walked Francesca to her bedroom and kissed her. On the way back to the kitchen he looked out the front window. The car was nowhere in sight. He hoped he never saw the woman again.

*　　*　　*

Annie was the first one up in the morning. She woke her mother and grandmother, then ran down the stairs to wake Rudolfo. She knocked on his door and then barged in, "Rudy, get up, it's time to go to New York." She turned on the light. "Rudy, where are you?"

"I'm in here, Annie," called Rudolfo from the bathroom.

She ran to the bathroom door, looked at what he was doing, then pointed to his face. "You look funny with that white cream. I gotta go get dressed." She went to the stairs, turned around and yelled, "Mom said we can have breakfast at the airport," then ran up the stairs.

*   *   *

Standing in line at the airport, Annie was fascinated by everything—all the people, the big counters at the airline checkpoints, and the airplanes that she saw through the large windows. Rudolfo picked her up and instructed her on how to get his boarding pass while Francesca and Rose were checking in. She pushed the buttons on the machine, scanned his passport, and then reached down and took out his boarding ticket. The agent took Rudolfo's luggage, gave him his claim check, and proceeded to check Annie in.

Before entering security, Rudolfo told Annie that she needed to take off her coat and shoes, and remove anything metal from her pockets before going through security. "Do I have to take off my shoes, Rudy?"

"Yes, everyone does."

She sat down on the floor, untied her shoes, took them off, then stood and took off her coat. "Okay, I'm ready to go through."

"Where are you traveling, young lady?" asked the security guard.

"I'm going to New York to see Rudy's family."

"Who's Rudy?"

She held Rudy's leg, "Rudy is my dad, I mean my friend."

"Have a safe trip."

They purchased breakfast and took the bags of food to their gate. "This is cool, Mommy, sitting in these chairs and eating."

"Yeah, cool," said Francesca. "Are you having fun so far?"

Annie took a bite of her breakfast sandwich, then said, "Yeah, this is fun. I can't wait to get on the plane."

"I'm going to go to the rest room," said Rudolfo. "I'll be right back."

While he was washing his hands, he was thinking of the woman again. It's good we are leaving the state, he thought, so Annie will be safe. Then he thought of Annie calling him dad and how that touched his heart. For the short amount of time he had been in Minnesota, they had been inseparable.

On his way back to the gate, he noticed Rose and Francesca, but he didn't see Annie. He ran the rest of the way. "Where's Annie? Weren't you watching her?"

Annie stood up. She was sitting on the floor by Rose, coloring. Rudolfo picked her up. "You scared me. I thought you disappeared." He set her down on the chair next to him. "You stay here by me." He put Annie's coloring book and colors in her backpack and set the backpack on the chair next to her.

Francesca looked at Rose, who had a look on her face that matched Francesca's confusion. Francesca didn't know why Rudolfo was so shaken, but she would find out as soon as they were alone. Annie didn't seem affected, just happy that he wanted her to sit by him.

$$* \quad * \quad *$$

Annie's designated seat was next to Rose's on the flight to New York, but Rudolfo insisted that she sit by him, so Rose and Francesca sat together, one row back, and Francesca wasn't able to talk to Rudolfo.

At one point during the flight, Annie wanted to be with her mother. Rose and Annie traded seats, and as soon as Annie got to her new seat she put on her seat belt.

"Hi, Mom."

"Do you like flying?"

"It's neat." She wiggled in her seat to get comfortable. "I forgot my books—can I go get them?"

"Why don't you just stay here for now? We'll be landing in an hour."

"Do you have some paper and a pencil?"

Francesca had learned early to carry those things for her daughter. Annie always wanted to draw or practice writing.

While Annie was drawing, Francesca looked out the window. She thought that Rudolfo was just being careful and that she shouldn't question why, but then she'd never seen him like that before. However, in the seat in front of her, her mother was trying to get all the details from Rudolfo.

"Are you all right, Rudolfo?"

"Yes, why?"

"You were so worried about Annie at the airport."

"I want her first flight to be a good one." He continued to look out the window.

"By panicking?"

He turned to look at Rose. "I know I overreacted. Something happened yesterday in the grocery store that has made me worried about Annie's safety."

Rudolfo's statement affected Rose's whole being, and she felt herself starting to panic. "What do you mean?" she whispered.

"I want to tell Francesca, but I don't want her to worry." He waited until the flight attendant had passed by, then continued with what had happened in the grocery store.

"No! Tell me it's not true." Rose tried to keep her voice from quivering.

"She's okay with all of us watching her. I've been looking at the passengers, and I don't see the woman who was in the grocery store."

"That's good news," Rose said. She looked at Rudolfo. "This will devastate Francesca when she finds out. But you need to tell her as soon as you can."

"I know."

Chapter Twelve

Carmella's husband, Tony, was at the airport waiting for Rudolfo and his guests to arrive. Carmella had been apprehensive about her brother's finding a new lady, and now they were finally going to meet her. Tony remembered Rudolfo's last two lady friends. As soon as Carmella had met them she had known the relationships wouldn't last. In each case the outcome had been devastating to Rudolfo.

Tony feared it was going to happen a third time. When he and Carmella talked about it, they tried to be optimistic and positive that Francesca was the one for Rudolfo. They would soon find out. One thing they knew for sure was that their children were excited about Uncle Rudolfo coming to New York. Especially Giovanni, who still hadn't revealed where he wanted to go with his uncle and what he wanted Rudolfo to paint. I guess this week will be full of surprises, thought Tony.

*　　*　　*

Rudolfo hugged his brother-in-law, then introduced Francesca, Annie, and Rose. They collected their luggage and put it in Tony's van. Then Rudolfo helped the three ladies into the back seat and made sure they were buckled in. He got in front with his brother-in-law, and they talked all the way to Tony and Carmella's home.

Once they were inside the large house, Carmella hugged her brother and kissed him on the cheek. She said something in Italian, and Rudolfo responded in Italian and let out a loud laugh.

All at once, the De Luca children ran to Rudolfo, chattering in Italian, except for Giovanni. He stood looking up at the uncle he'd never seen but had heard a lot about in the last month. Rudolfo picked him up and said, "This must be Giovanni," then kissed his nephew on both cheeks.

"You are going to paint me a picture?" asked Giovanni, shyly, getting excited that he could finally tell his uncle what he wanted.

"Yes," Rudolfo looked around, "but first I want you to meet my friends."

He put Giovanni down and introduced everyone. Carmella was amazed that he remembered her children's names. If he moves to Minnesota, maybe he'll visit more often, she found herself hoping.

After all the luggage was brought in and they were shown to their rooms, Rudolfo went to Francesca's room. Annie and Rose were sitting on the bed. He looked at Rose, and she knew this was her cue. "Annie, let's go to your room and unpack," she said.

As soon as they left the room, Rudolfo told Francesca, "I need to talk to you about something." He touched her shoulders. "I know this won't be pleasant, but you need to know."

"What is it? You're scaring me."

"Let's sit down."

They sat in the corner in the two brown plush chairs. Francesca hoped that what he was about to tell her was why he had acted the way he had in the airport.

Rudolfo was careful how he told the story, but he told her everything up to the time when Francesca had come home the night before and the woman had left.

"Oh, my God!" If anything happened to Annie, Francesca knew she would die inside. Rudolfo's story was much different than the ones she had created in her mind after the incident at the airport.

Rudolfo went to her and pulled her into his arms. "What are we going to do?" asked Francesca. "I don't want Annie hurt."

"I feel that she is safe in New York. When we get back to Minnesota I won't let her out of my sight. If I see the woman again, I'll call the police."

"I know she'll be safe with you." Tears ran down Francesca's face, and Rudolfo held her tight. "I just don't know what we'll do once she starts back to school."

"By, then," said Rudolfo with confidence, "the woman will be caught."

*   *   *

Carmella made her famous spaghetti and also tiramisu, as she always had in the past on the first day her brother arrived at their home. After they were all seated and grace was said, Rudolfo reminded his nieces and nephews that their guests didn't speak much Italian. Annie looked at Rudolfo.

"Except Annie," Rudolfo said. "She's been teaching me English and I've been teaching her Italian." He winked at Annie, "She learns more quickly than I do."

Looking at his nieces and nephews, his heart swelled with pride. Now Annie was in his life, and he was equally proud of her. How wonderful it would be to have children with Francesca, and have Annie as their sister, he thought. He looked around the long table. Maria was helping Annie with some Italian sentences. Giovanni, on Annie's other side, interrupted her by whispering something in her ear. She giggled, and Giovanni wore a wide smile on his face.

The three of them got up from the table. Carmella said, "You two have kitchen duty—don't go running off."

"Can Annie help us?" asked Maria.

"No, she's a guest. Guests don't do the dishes."

"I want to help," Annie blurted out.

"When we are done we want to talk to Uncle Rudy," said Giovanni.

"You can find me on the porch," said Rudolfo. When visiting his sister, sitting on the porch was his favorite thing to do.

*   *   *

Rose was picked up by her friend, Jerry. The kitchen duty trio started clearing off the table as Carmella brought coffee and tiramisu out to the porch. The other four children put on their winter jackets and went to their neighbor's house and knocked. Several minutes later, three more children came out and joined the De Lucas in their fenced-in backyard.

The porch was on the front of the house. Francesca chose a recliner to sit in, very similar to the one Rudolfo had in his living room in Florence. Rudolfo sat in the rocking chair next to her, and Tony and Carmella sat on the couch across from them. Through the large porch windows they could see the neighbors coming and going.

Giovanni rushed to the porch with Annie and Maria following. "Uncle, Uncle, we're ready to talk to you."

Annie went to her mother. "Mom, look, my hands are all wrinkly."

Francesca took Annie's hands and turned them over. "How did that happen?" asked Francesca, knowing full well what her daughter had been doing.

"I washed the dishes. It's funner than wiping them." She kissed her mom. "I gotta go, we're talking to Rudy about . . . um, I can't tell you. Bye, Mom."

Giovanni led the way to his bedroom. Annie made sure that she caught up with Rudolfo and took his hand. He looked down at her and smiled.

* * *

"If you'll excuse me," said Tony, "I'll go check on the children."

Francesca and Carmella were left alone on the porch. Francesca was nervous. She didn't know what to say. Ever since they had arrived at the De Luca's home, she felt that Carmella had been watching her.

Once her husband left, Carmella didn't waste any time. "My brother has told me how you two met." She smiled, putting Francesca at ease. "You stepped on his feet."

"Yes, but I found out he was looking for me all the time," Francesca said. She took a sip of coffee. "Sometimes it seems like a fantasy, but I know it's real."

"He loves you." Carmella looked away, composed her thoughts, and then focused on Francesca. "I worry about that." She didn't let Francesca respond. "Two other women Rudolfo thought he loved turned out to be disastrous relationships. I didn't think he'd recover from the last woman he dated."

"What happened?" asked Francesca. Rudolfo had told her a little about the women he had been with but he hadn't given much detail.

"I'll start with Julie, the first woman. She wanted Rudolfo to quit his career and find a corporate job that would pay lots of money so she wouldn't have to work. Rudolfo told her no, he loved what he did. Julie told him he'd better be rich, then, or she wouldn't continue to date him. Filipo called one day saying that my brother couldn't pay the rent and asking if I could send some money. He promised me he would say it was his money so Rudolfo didn't know I was involved."

"Did you ever find out what happened?" Francesca asked.

"Julie said she wanted his money to invest so she could double it and then they could get married. Rudolfo loved her and of course let her have his money. One day she came to his apartment and told him that the stock market didn't do too well, and she lost his money."

Carmella tucked her legs under her and took a sip of coffee. "The coffee is cold—would you like me to warm it?"

"No, thank you. Please, continue your story."

"He told her to leave his apartment and he would call her the next day. He went over there instead. The landlord said she had packed her things the night before and left. She was going to Siena to buy a house."

Francesca felt anger surge through her body. "How can people be so heartless?"

"I don't know. I just wished my brother wasn't a part of it."

After finishing her tiramisu, Carmella continued. "Then there was Tina. They talked about children. She was open to the idea but wasn't sure, and that's when Rudolfo thought a trip to New York to see his nieces and nephews would change her mind—help her decide to have children. They were here a week. Tina left one day to go shopping and came back late in the evening. She had many packages, so no one thought anything of it."

Carmella sipped her coffee even though it was cold. "Once back in Florence," she continued, "Rudolfo asked her to marry him. She said yes and she said she wanted children. That made him so happy that he called me after she left that night. It was four o'clock in the morning."

Carmella went on. "Two days before the wedding Rudolfo tried to contact her, but she didn't answer her phone and didn't return his calls. He thought she might be busy getting ready for the wedding. Tony and I were staying with Filipo, and we tried to reassure Rudolfo things would work out.

"We all went to the church, but Tina never showed up. She broke his heart. A month later he received a letter from her saying she went back to New York, started a new job, and fell in love with her manager, someone who understood her. She thanked Rudolfo for taking her to New York. The day she went shopping, she was also looking for a job."

Carmella sighed. "He tried to cope with the situation, and I thought he was until Filipo called me and told me to come to Italy, 'Rudy not doing so good.'"

"I had no idea it was that bad," said Francesca as tears formed in her eyes.

"So you can see now why I don't trust you."

Francesca had not been prepared for what Carmella had just said. She would not cry and show her that she was weak, and when the anger lessened, she said, "I mean Rudolfo no harm." Francesca took a sip from her cup, then continued to tell Carmella about Annie's father. "I told myself I would never get close to anyone ever again, especially not love again, but Rudolfo came into my life and things changed. Annie loves him. You have children. Would you let your children get attached to someone and then just leave?"

Francesca felt her body get warm as the anger was returning. "I don't think you would. I have no intention of taking his money or leaving him at the altar. I especially don't like the way you thought I was already going to betray him before I even arrived at your home. If you don't believe me when I tell you I love him, please believe that Annie does."

"I can tell by the way she always holds his hand," Carmella said.

"How can you say you don't trust me?" asked Francesca. "I should wonder if I can trust Rudolfo. He might be getting revenge for the past loves that failed. Once we set a date he might leave me at the altar."

"My brother is too kindhearted, he would never want revenge," said Carmella.

"Nor would I." Francesca looked away, tired of defending herself.

After several minutes of silence, Carmella spoke and Francesca looked at her. "I like you, Francesca, don't get me wrong. After our talk I believe you are not out to hurt my brother." Then she smiled. "But I had to find out." She stood and picked up the dishes. "We'll have a wonderful Christmas. I received the presents you sent and hid them right away. I knew the children couldn't resist opening them."

Carmella left the room and Francesca was alone, glad their talk was over, and the air was cleared. Rudolfo had gone through a lot, and she planned to make up for all the hurt he had suffered, and maybe she would heal, also, from her bad relationship.

She felt empty after Carmella had accused her of things that weren't true, and she needed to talk to Rudofo, feel him next to her and wished he would come back to the porch and be with her again. Being alone with him had been rare during the month of December. Hopefully that will change once we get back to Minnesota, she thought.

Chapter Thirteen

The next day, Rudolfo, Maria, Giovanni, and Annie headed north on foot down the sidewalk in front of the De Luca home. Rudolfo had his easels tucked under his arm, and each child had a container of paints and brushes.

"Giovanni, when will you tell me where we are going?"

"It's still a secret, Uncle Rudy."

"He hasn't even told me, and I'm his sister," said Maria.

Annie smiled. He had told her, but she had promised not to tell.

After they had walked several blocks, Giovanni pointed to a brick building. "Hey, everybody! We're going to that building." The building had "FIRE HOUSE" engraved on the front.

Giovanni walked right in the side door as if he'd done it many times before, and the others followed. "Ah, Giovanni, I didn't see you yesterday," said the fire captain.

"Mom said we had to clean our rooms because our uncle was coming."

"Maria, it's good to see you again." They did a high five. "The last time we met you had just started taking piano lessons."

"Yes, sir." She looked at the floor. "But . . . I'm not practicing every day like I'm supposed to."

He patted her on the head. "You're a smart kid, you'll figure it out." Maria looked up at him and smiled.

The man shook Rudolfo's hand. "I'm Captain Ellis. Please call me Jim."

"Has my nephew explained why I am here?"

"He told me several months ago and he's been stopping by ever since."

Rudolfo set down his easels and introduced Annie.

Captain Ellis shook Annie's hand. "Hi, Captain, I mean Jim."

"Calling me Captain is good, too." He looked at Annie's hair. "My, my, how did you get all that curly hair?"

Annie shrugged her shoulders, and said, "From my mom, I guess." She looked around the station, mesmerized by the big red fire trucks. "How come everyone has their coats hanging on all those hooks?"

Giovanni chimed in, "For the firemen when they go to fires. They put on their own coats, hop on the trucks, and go put out the fire." He pointed to the ladders on the trucks. "They use those in case they have to rescue people." He went up to the captain and whispered, "Do you have things all set up?"

"I sure do," said the Captain. "I'll take you all out the back door." He picked up the easels and led the way into a heated building behind the fire station. In it was a yellow 1941 fire truck.

After Captain Ellis gave a short history, Giovanni blurted out, "Can you paint that, Uncle Rudy?!"

"I sure can," said Rudolfo. "I just need some time to set up."

"I want you to paint two pictures." He looked at the fire truck. "One of the truck, and one of the truck with me and Maria. Can you do that? Oh, wait. Annie, too."

"Your brothers and sisters have only one painting."

"But Mom said she wasn't going to have any more children. So you paint two for me. Okay?"

Rudolfo laughed. "Okay. Which one do you want me to paint first?"

"Paint the fire truck first. The captain and some other firemen are giving us a tour, and then he goes home for lunch. He already said we could be here when he's gone, we just can't be inside the station."

Rudolfo smiled to himself. His nephew had done a lot of planning for this event, and he was so happy that Annie had been included. Alone in the backyard of the station, he studied the fire truck and the background, and then began painting.

*   *   *

Francesca and Rose were sitting on the porch. Rudolfo was still at the fire station. Rose was telling her daughter all about her friend Jerry. "His wife died two years ago, he's retired, and has two grandsons. His only son lives twenty miles away."

"Does he want to see you again?" Francesca asked.

"He wants me to go to a company party. Even though he's retired, he gets invited every year." She felt as if their roles were reversed. "So I need to go shopping." They both laughed.

"Funny, Mom." Francesca got up. "I need to check with Carmella to see if she needs me to do anything to get ready for Christmas."

"Invite her to come with us."

Several minutes later Carmella and Francesca came out to the porch. "I would love to go shopping," said Carmella. "I haven't bought myself anything new for a long, long time. It will take me a couple of minutes to get ready."

They could hear Carmella calling to Tony, "I'm going shopping." She told him where the children were. "We'll pick up something for supper," she added on the way out the door.

*   *   *

Rudolfo had finished one painting of the fire truck, and now after doing the second one it was time to paint the three children into the picture. However, when they were ready to pose, Captain Ellis brought lunch. "My wife knew you were all coming today so she made sandwiches and her famous chocolate chip cookies." He set up five chairs around the table behind the antique fire truck, and joined them at the table.

*   *   *

The three women stopped for lunch at a hometown Italian restaurant before they went shopping. Carmella ordered in Italian. "It's what I always order here—I'm sure you both will enjoy it."

Carmella told stories about herself and Rudolfo as they were growing up. "He would never fight with me. I yelled at him and punched him, but he would never fight back. One day when I was picking on him, I was on my way to camp. It had just stopped raining. I had my suitcase packed and sitting outside by the door. I told him that I wouldn't miss him and that Mom and Dad liked me best because I could go to camp and he couldn't. After ten minutes of that, he calmly picked up my suitcase, opened it, and dumped my clothes in the mud puddle in our driveway."

They all laughed. "What happened next?" asked Francesca.

"I was so startled that he did something that I started to laugh and I couldn't stop. Luckily I had enough clothes that I could repack. I never picked on him again."

The waiter brought breadsticks and salad to the table. When he left, Carmella added, "From that day on, we became very close. One year we even went to camp together."

Rose said, "Francesca, being an only child, didn't have anyone to pick on. Our neighbor had a little girl, and those two would play all day long and even sleep over at each other's houses. They were inseparable."

As they ate, they talked about the stores where Carmella thought Rose could find a hot dress to wear to the party. Rose didn't think she was hot and didn't think a dress would change that. But she was wrong. After going to several stores they found a mid-length, dark red dress that fit Rose's slim figure perfectly.

Francesca and Carmella picked out a gold chain and gold earrings for Rose to wear with the dress. Before they left, Carmella found a black dress. After trying it on, she purchased it. "Now I just have to convince Tony to take me out. I don't remember the last time we got away on our own."

"Go out tonight. Rudolfo and I will stay with the children," Francesca said.

"I couldn't ask you to do that."

"You don't have to, I've already volunteered."

Carmella hugged Francesca, "Yes, we'll go tonight."

When they left the store, Carmella led them across the street to a shoe store. "I forgot about shoes!" said Rose.

*   *   *

The two little girls kept giggling, which made Rudolfo smile. Even Giovanni was enjoying watching his new friend having so much fun. "Annie, you stand by me, but you have to stop giggling so Uncle can paint us." He looked at Maria, "You have to stop, too."

"You can keep laughing, just don't move," instructed Rudolfo. That made even Giovanni laugh.

*   *   *

On the way home, Carmella drove into McDonald's and picked up supper. "I'm surprised you eat at McDonald's," said Rose, "since you are such a good cook."

"Even cooks take a break once in a while, and besides the kids love it here. I buy everyone the same thing, that way I never get the wrong thing." Rose and Francesca chipped in to help pay for the burgers. "Except Rudolfo, he doesn't like McDonald's. He can eat leftovers," said Carmella, laughing.

Chapter Fourteen

Once the burgers and fries were eaten, Rudolfo and Francesca gave Caterina and Franco the night off from kitchen duty. The paintings hadn't yet been revealed. Giovanni was waiting for his mom and dad to come out of the bedroom before he showed them to everyone.

*   *   *

"Francesca," said Rose, "I'm so nervous." She tried putting on her gold chain. "Here," she handed her daughter the necklace, "you put it on."

"You look great, Mom." There was a knock on the door. "Come in!"

Annie opened the door. "Grandma, you're all dressed up. Are you wearing red for Christmas?"

"I guess I am. Do I look okay, Annie?"

"You look nice, Grandma. Are you going on a date? When Mom dressed up in her black dress, she went out with Rudy."

"Yes, I have a date. His name is Jerry."

"Are you getting married?"

Rose smiled, "No, I'm not getting married."

"When you do, will Jerry be my grandpa?"

"Annie," said Francesca gently, "Grandma is only going to a party with Jerry, that's all."

"Okay. Are you both ready to see the paintings?"

"We'll be down in a minute," said Francesca.

Annie closed the door behind her. "Does that mean Jerry will be my dad?" Rose threw a pillow at her daughter.

"I'm only going on a date!"

*   *   *

All the children were sitting on the long couch in the living room, waiting for the adults to come in so Giovanni could reveal his paintings. None of them minded that their uncle had painted two pictures for their youngest brother and only one for them.

Rudolfo and Francesca arrived first and sat down on the plush green loveseat across from the children. Tony and Carmella were the next to arrive. Tony had on a dark blue suit, a white shirt, and a paisley tie. Carmella wore her new black dress and had her hair swept up and clipped in the back.

Caterina and Maria went to their mother. Caterina spoke first. "Mom, where are you going? You look really nice."

Maria took Carmella's hand. "Can I come with you?"

Caterina, now eleven, said to her younger sister, "I think Mom and Dad want to be alone tonight." She looked at her parents. "Right, Mom?"

"That's right."

Antonio, Mario, Franco, and Giovanni were by their dad, asking him questions all at once. "Where are you going?" "Don't you want to see the picture?" "Can we come with?" "How come you're going without us?"

"Your parents need some time by themselves," said Rudolfo, "so Francesca and I are going to stay here to make sure you all behave."

"Come on, Uncle Rudy, you know we are good kids," said Antonio, the oldest.

Rudolfo smiled. As a child, whenever he had done something he was not supposed to be doing, and Carmella had found out, she told on him every time. He suspected that with his nieces and nephews it was the same way and that they didn't get by with much or try to very often.

When they were all seated again, Rose entered the room. Annie went right over to her. "Isn't my Grandma pretty?"

"I don't have a grandma," said Franco. "Can she be mine, too?"

"Grandma, Grandma, can you be Franco's grandma, too?"

Rose looked at Carmella. Carmella said, "Our parents passed away when Rudolfo and I were in our twenties. Tony's parents died last year in an auto accident."

"Grandma, will you?" Carmella nodded at Rose.

"Of course I will," Rose said. Franco gave her a hug as the other children watched. One by one they all went up to Rose and gave a hug to their new grandmother. Rose had tears in her eyes.

Annie spoke again. "My grandma, I mean our grandma, has a date. She's going out with Jerry."

"Let's wait for Jerry to come so we can show him the paintings, too," said Giovanni. Just then the doorbell rang.

Last year Tony had put on an addition to the living room, and now he was glad that he had. Tony and Carmella sat in the chairs next to Francesca and Rudolfo, while Rose answered the door.

"Rose, you look beautiful," Jerry said. He held her at arm's length. "Let me look at you." He was about to embrace her when he heard giggling. He looked into the room and saw all the children. He whispered to Rose, "You look very beautiful."

Jerry had white hair, was six feet tall, and slim. His black suit and white shirt accented his dark tan. The red in his tie matched Rose's dress.

Rose and Jerry took the last two chairs and sat and waited with the rest of them. Rudolfo helped Giovanni carry the paintings into the living room. Giovanni held the first one, almost touching the floor, so his mom and dad could see first, and then he slowly turned it around so everyone could see.

"Giovanni, I didn't know you liked fire trucks," said his mother.

"I do, Mom. I want to be a fireman some day. Wait, we have one more."

He unveiled the second painting in the same manner. It was the same fire truck but with three giggly children standing in front of it. They had their arms around each other as if they were holding each other up. There was a tear in Maria's eye. While she explained that it was from giggling so hard, she and Annie started laughing.

"Where are you going to hang them, Giovanni?" asked Mario.

"I don't know yet."

Jerry and Rose stood up. "We'd better go. We don't want to be late." Jerry helped Rose with her coat.

"I want you home by midnight," said Rudolfo.

"I'll do my best, but she's a stubborn woman," said Jerry, smiling.

Everyone yelled, "Good-bye, Grandma" as Rose and Jerry left.

"We'd better be going, too, Carmella."

"Rudolfo, if you can get them to stay on the couch, paint them. I would love to have the painting hanging right here in this room," Carmella said. She gave her brother and Francesca hugs, then looked at her children. "You all be good," she told them. Then she said something in Italian and they all laughed.

Rudolfo whispered to Francesca. "She told them I would tell on them if they were naughty."

*　　*　　*

"Derek, this is my friend, Rose. We met in college and haven't seen each other for quite some time."

Derek shook hands with Rose. "Jerry worked for our law firm for over twenty years," he said. "We like to have him back here each Christmas because we're keeping tabs on him in case he wants to come back to work for us."

"That won't happen," interjected Jerry. "I'm too busy with my grandkids."

Derek pointed toward the food, "As always, there is plenty to eat." He took Rose's hand. "It's good to meet you," he said. "Now if you'll excuse me, I have to welcome some more guests."

"I think we should skip the food and go to my place," whispered Jerry.

"We just got here. I'm starving, unless you have good food like this at your house."

"Okay, let's eat. Then can we go?"

*   *   *

Tony and Carmella were sitting at a corner table at their favorite Italian restaurant. They had just finished eating and were pondering what they should order for dessert.

"Carmella, you look beautiful in your new dress." Tony took her hand. "I know you are very busy with our children during the day while I work, and I really appreciate all you do." He leaned in and kissed her. "I love you."

"I love you, too," Carmella said. She touched the front of his shirt. "You look good in a suit."

He kissed her again.

"I think we should stay in the city, get a hotel, and play hooky for a couple more days. You're brother is here—he can manage the children," suggested Tony.

"I like the part about playing hooky, but I don't know about Rudolfo managing or wanting to for any longer than tonight. But we can stay here for a while longer. I like being alone with you."

*   *   *

The children were all seated on the couch as Rudolfo painted them. The younger children kept squirming, while the older ones were making funny faces. Rudolfo painted their bodies without their faces. He was waiting until they calmed down. He wanted the painting to look right for his sister.

Francesca was in the kitchen making a snack. She had decided to make popcorn, but had no idea how much to make for nine people. The kettle had oil in it, and when the first kernel popped she added more and put on the lid.

Suddenly Annie was pulling on Francesca's shirt. "Mommy, Mommy, something happened to Rudy." Francesca turned off the heat and in a panic followed her daughter to Rudolfo.

*   *   *

"This is much nicer," Rose said, sipping her drink. "Your friends are nice, but it was getting rowdy."

"With a room full of lawyers it's bound to get noisy. We all want to outdo each other." Jerry looked at Rose. "God, it's good to see you again. How long will you be staying?"

"We will be going home," she had to stop and think, "January second."

He let out a sigh. "I was hoping you'd be here for New Year's."

"What do you have in mind?" She smiled at him.

"My son, his wife and grandsons come over and we watch videos and overeat. I hope you say yes that you'll join us. Annie can come, too."

"I can't see it as a problem, but I really should check with Francesca first. Annie is having so much fun with all the children, I don't know if she'll want to be away from them, unless we invite them all over here."

"Whoa, that's a lot of kids in one house." He laughed. "I'll have to think about that."

Rose and Jerry were enjoying each other's company as they sat in front of the fireplace and talked about Rose's next visit to New York. Jerry put his arm around her, and she could feel the warmth of his body. With the wine, and the late hour, they decided to just enjoy the moment of being together.

*   *   *

Rose arrived back at the De Luca home first. What surprised her was that all the lights seemed to be on. She had assumed she would be able to walk in and go to her room without her daughter asking any questions. But it was not her daughter waiting at the kitchen table; it was a neighbor.

"You must be Rose," the woman said. She got up from her chair. "I'm Sylvia. I live across the street."

"What happened?! Is everyone all right?"

"The children are all here. Rudolfo was sick; Francesca called an ambulance and then called me. Francesca and Annie took my car and followed the ambulance to the hospital."

"Oh, no." Rose sat down. "He was sick before he came to America. But he was vague about what had happened. I hope he's okay." Her daughter loved Rudolfo, and if anything happened to him she knew Francesca would not have an easy time of it. Nor would Annie. "Annie! How is she handling it?" she asked.

"She started crying when the ambulance came, as did some of the other children, and Annie wanted to ride with him, but the paramedics explained how important it was that she went with her mom, and she could see Rudy at the hospital."

Rose clutched her chest.

Carmella and Tony arrived minutes after Rose. "Sylvia, what's going on?" asked Carmella. Sylvia explained what had happened in greater detail, as she knew that Carmella would want to know everything. She recounted that Rudolfo had broken out in a sweat and passed out on the floor, and then the ambulance had been called.

"Sylvia…" but Carmella didn't get the words out before Sylvia interrupted.

"Go to the hospital. I'll stay here all night if need be."

110

Carmella hugged her, tears streaming down her face. "Thanks, Sylvia."

Carmella, Tony and Rose headed to the hospital with the same guilt feeling for being selfish, and staying out as long as they could when they should have been home with their families. Carmella was thinking about Rudolfo's first attack and remembering how she had thought that they might lose him. She knew she had to convince her brother to tell Francesca what was wrong. After all, they were to marry, and it would only be fair that she knew.

Chapter Fifteen

Annie was sitting on her mom's lap, trying to stay awake, but eventually she fell asleep. It had been over an hour, and the doctor still hadn't come out to talk to Francesca. She wondered how Rudolfo was doing. Was this the same thing that had happened to him before he came to America? Rudolfo hadn't given her a lot of information when she had asked him about it, but she had assumed that he was well now—until tonight.

The thought of losing him crossed her mind more than once—and Annie, what about Annie? She had found someone she wanted as her father, and what if he . . . she couldn't get herself to say the word. When Annie was crying tonight, it had been more than Francesca could bear. She had never before felt such pain.

She had to change her thoughts. Rudolfo will recover, we will get married, and Annie will have a father. She had to tell herself that—if not for herself, for Annie.

Francesca looked at the clock as she'd been doing ever since they had arrived at the hospital. It was one in the morning. She was exhausted, but her love for Rudolfo kept her going. As soon as Annie woke up, Francesca thought, she would look for some coffee.

"Francesca," said Rose.

"Mom!" The tears started again.

"Let me take Annie." She reached down and picked up the sleeping child, then sat down with her.

"Francesca," said Carmella, "come with us. We'll try and find out how he's doing."

Francesca was relieved that the others were with her at the hospital; she didn't feel so alone. Francesca followed them down the hall to the nurse's station. Without waiting for someone to look up, Carmella spoke first. "Excuse me, I want to know how my brother is doing. Rudolph Vittori. He was brought in by ambulance."

The nurse looked up his name on the computer. "The doctor should be out any time now."

"Can't you tell me anything right now?"

"No, it would be best if you waited for the doctor."

Tony took his wife's hand and led her away from the desk. "Carmella, they are doing the best they can. We'll go back to the waiting room and wait for the doctor."

Reluctantly she turned, and the three went back to join Rose and Annie.

Another hour passed, and the doctor still hadn't come to talk to them. Carmella paced back and forth in the waiting area. Several times she told Tony she was going to find the doctor, but Tony convinced her that the doctor probably needed to be with Rudolfo right now. That calmed her down until the next time she was up and pacing and Tony had to remind her again.

Annie was awake, sitting in her grandmother's lap, sucking her thumb and twirling her hair—something she hadn't done since she was two. Her eyes were red from crying and lack of sleep. She took out her thumb and asked her mother for money to buy food from the machines. Francesca gave her some and Annie crawled out of Rose's lap. "I can do it by myself, Mom," she said, and took off down the hall.

Except she didn't stop at the machines, she kept walking down the hall and looked into each room as she went. She spotted Rudolfo and went into the room. There were no doctors or nurses around him, so she went to his bed.

*   *   *

"Annie should be back by now; the machines are just down the hall," said Francesca in a worried voice. She thought about what Rudolfo told her about the woman in Minnesota and she panicked with what viable senses she had left. "I'm going to look for her."

"I'm coming, too," said Carmella, eager to be doing something besides pacing the floor.

They found the machines, then continued as Annie had, looking in each room until they found her. Carmella's hand went to her mouth. Francesca was having the same reaction. They went over to the bed. Annie was lying beside Rudolfo with her arm around him.

Neither stirred as the two women stood and watched. Francesca thought that Annie looked more at peace at this moment than she had all night. Tears formed in Francesca's eyes at the thought of Rudolfo not making it, and about how a heartbroken little girl would have to try to sort out the facts of life at such an early age.

"Can I help?"

They turned around to see a male doctor standing behind them. "Yes, you can help," spoke Carmella. "How is my brother?"

"He's had quite a time of it," said the doctor, "did you know he has had malaria?"

"Yes, I knew." She avoided looking at Francesca, thinking she should have explained this to her and Rose. "What are you doing for him?"

"We've put him on different medication. The card he carries in his wallet was very helpful. It appears he had a relapse not long ago." The doctor looked at Annie for the first time. "You will have to take her out of here; your brother is very sick and she shouldn't be here."

Carmella had read extensively about malaria when her brother was first diagnosed after his trip to Africa. She knew that in humans, malaria is transmitted only by anopheline mosquitoes. She knew that Annie was safe lying there, and she also knew that the comfort of a child, one he loved, would be the best medicine.

"From what I understand about malaria, Annie's not at risk. So I would like her to stay. Francesca and I will also stay until you can tell us more about his progress. I know it's hard to tell right away, so we will stay until there is improvement." Carmella looked at her brother, then faced the doctor. "Can we get more chairs? My husband and Annie's grandmother are in the waiting room, and they would like to be here also." She turned quickly around as if to dismiss him from the room.

Several minutes later chairs were brought in, and Rose and Tony joined them. Rose went over and touched Annie's face. Rudolfo was so pale next to her. Tubes were going into his arm and wires were on his chest, but Annie seemed to have missed all the cords and tubes and was snuggled into his body.

Once they were all seated, Carmella explained to Rose and Francesca that Rudolfo had been asked to go to Africa to paint and write about the culture. "He was there several weeks. A month after he returned to Italy he was in the hospital with a fever and chills. The doctors diagnosed him and he was fine for a while, but then it reoccurred. This is the fourth recurrence. During that time no one has changed his medication. Hopefully with his new medicine he'll never have to go through this again."

Sensing that Francesca might have felt hurt because Rudolfo had not told her about all this, she continued. "He didn't even tell me for a while. He's a proud man and didn't want anyone to know about what happened to him."

"Carmella straightened him out right away once she found out," said Tony. "She told him it was nothing to be ashamed of. I think he was more afraid of his sister than anything else."

For the first time since arriving at the hospital, they were able to laugh.

*   *   *

Sylvia was in the kitchen when the De Luca children came in for breakfast. Sylvia had only two children of her own, but she gauged how much pancake batter she would need and there was enough for everyone. Her husband Henry was there to help her. While he poured six glasses of milk, Mario put out the plates, silverware, and napkins.

"These pancakes are better than Mom's," commented Antonio, with his mouth full.

Henry smiled and then sat down to eat. "Sylvia has always made good pancakes. That's why I married her."

The younger children giggled as they thought of the pancakes and of Henry getting married. Giovanni was quiet all through breakfast. Once the children had cleaned the kitchen and left to play, Giovanni stayed behind to talk to Henry.

"Mr. Ryan, do you know if Annie is okay?" He looked down at the table. "She was so sad when Uncle Rudy got sick."

Henry set his hand on Giovanni's. "I'm sure she's okay."

"Can we call the hospital to find out?"

"We sure can. Go get me the phone book."

Giovanni dragged his chair over to the counter, climbed up, and got the phone book out of the cupboard and threw it on the floor. Henry smiled again. Out of breath, Giovanni brought the book over to Henry, then ran and got the phone.

Henry dialed and waited for someone to answer. "I would like to talk to Carmella De Luca. She's probably with Rudolfo Vittori. He was taken there by ambulance."

"Just a minute, I'll connect you."

Several transfers later, he was able to talk to Carmella. "This is Henry. Your son wants to talk to you."

"Mom, is Annie okay? How is Uncle Rudy?" Giovanni was rubbing his foot on the floor. "Mom, is everyone okay?"

"Yes, dear, everyone is okay. Annie is with Uncle Rudy right now."

"Is she still sad?"

"Right now she's sleeping."

"Tell her 'hi' for me and that I'm worried about her. I want her to come home so we can talk about Uncle Rudy."

Surprised that her son sounded so grown up and also realizing how much he cared about his new friend, Carmella answered, "When she wakes up I'll have her call you. Will that be all right?"

A smile came to his face. "Okay, I'll hang up so the phone isn't busy so she can call."

"Wait, Giovanni! Let me talk to Mr. Ryan."

* * *

Even though Rudolfo was burning with fever, he felt content—unlike the last time when Filipo had been by his side in Florence. He remembered tossing and turning and feeling frantic about not being able to see Francesca. Now, he heard several familiar voices, but didn't know whose they were. Occasionally he felt something stir in his bed, but he knew that wasn't possible. He was on his side with his arm around something. To him it felt like the teddy bear he had had when he was a child, but the bear didn't squirm, and never whispered in his ear like this one did.

He heard the voices again, and thought one was close to his ear, but before he could open his eyes he fell back to sleep.

* * *

"I think we should go to the cafeteria and eat breakfast," said Carmella. "Rudolfo will be okay without us for a while."

Francesca didn't want to leave. What she really wanted to do was go over and sit next to Rudolfo's bed and hold his hand. With Carmella and Tony in the room, she didn't feel comfortable doing that.

"Francesca," said Rose gently, "do you want to eat?"

"I would rather stay here."

"We won't be gone long," said Carmella. "I'll go out to the front desk and see when the doctor is coming." Before Carmella got up, the doctor appeared in the doorway.

"Let's go where there will be some privacy," said the doctor, as he gestured to an empty room with several chairs.

Francesca and Carmella followed him, and when they were seated, the doctor explained to the women that Rudolfo was doing well. "The malaria seems to be taking its course faster than what I've experienced in patients."

"When can he come home?" asked Carmella. "It's only two more days until Christmas."

"If he keeps improving he'll be home by then. I'm concerned about his traveling." He looked at Rudolfo's chart. "He lives in Italy, doesn't he?"

"Yes, he does, but he'll be staying at my house, here in town. When he is able to travel he'll be going back to Minnesota."

"That's much closer than Italy, but I would wait at least a week. From looking at his chart he may have traveled too soon after his last attack. I'm sure that had a lot to do with his being in the hospital today."

He continued. "I wasn't going to mention this," he looked at Francesca, "but since your little girl crawled in bed with him, I feel that's the reason he's doing so well. She must really love her dad."

Francesca didn't correct him. "Yes, she does love him."

The doctor stood up. "You might as well get something to eat," he said. He looked back at Francesca. "I'm sure your daughter won't leave her dad's side, so I'll have the nurse bring her some food."

Carmella and Francesca were left alone in the small room. "I like the sound of that," remarked Carmella. "I'm sure Rudolfo would love to hear Annie call him Dad."

"Annie never met her dad, and she's really never asked, either." Francesca continued, "I do know that she really likes her friend Grace's dad." She took a tissue from the box on the windowsill and wiped her eyes. "Sometimes Annie goes with Grace and her family to their cabin on the weekends. When she gets home all she talks about is all the things Grace's dad did during the weekend. I feel bad that she doesn't have a dad that she can rely on and do things with."

"Rudolfo has already filled that void," said Carmella.

"Yes, he has." Francesca took another tissue. "When we first met I thought he wanted to get me to his apartment to harm me, so I wasn't going to meet him." Francesca touched Carmella's arm. "I'm glad I made the right decision."

"I am, too. Are you hungry yet?"

"Very hungry."

Chapter Sixteen

They were seated in the hospital cafeteria, with their food from the buffet, when Carmella spoke. "I never thought I'd be in this dress so long."

"It's starting to be uncomfortable," said Rose. "These shoes are hurting my feet." She slipped them off under the table and let out a sigh.

"Ladies, ladies," said Tony. "It's the price you pay for looking so beautiful."

"I'd rather be in jeans," said Rose, as she tugged on her dress.

"Of course you're both just as beautiful in jeans."

"Nice try, dear, but it's too late."

"I'm in trouble now." Tony laughed. "I hope Rudolfo gets well soon. It's tough being the only male."

*　　*　　*

Annie was rubbing Rudolfo's face with her hands as she whispered, "Wake up, Rudy, you gotta wake up."

After several attempts, she sat on the side of the bed and started to eat the soup the nurse had brought her. She wanted to save some for Rudolfo, but the nurse told her he would have his own food when he woke up.

As she was eating, Annie looked at the tray table and saw a piece of paper with her name on it. It read, "Annie, call Giovanni" and listed the number.

Annie looked around, and saw a phone on the nightstand next to the bed. She reached carefully for the phone so as not to spill her soup. She put the phone in her lap, dialed the number, and waited.

"Annie, is that you?" answered Giovanni, breathing heavily from running to the phone.

"Yes, it's Annie."

"What took you so long to call? Are you okay? Where are you?"

"I'm with Rudy and he's sleeping."

"Are you still sad?"

"Not anymore. I sneaked away from Mom and Grandma and crawled in bed with Rudy."

"Okay, hurry home. Arrivederci!"

"Giovanni, wait!"

"What?"

"Do you think Rudy would mind if I called him Dad?"

"He is your dad, right? So you should call him Dad."

"Okay, bye," said Annie, and hung up.

*   *   *

Smells of ham, baked bread, and Italian sausage were coming from the De Luca kitchen on Christmas Eve morning. Rose was helping Carmella in the kitchen, and it amazed Rose how helpful children could be. Each child had specific duties. Two peeled the potatoes, two set the table, two made salads. When they were done with these duties, there were new ones waiting for them. Rose noticed that not one child complained—although she did find it hard to imagine anyone arguing with Carmella and winning.

Carmella even put Annie to work, but Annie informed Carmella that she was going to the hospital to pick up her dad and that her jobs might not get done. Carmella smiled at her and hugged her close. "I love you, Annie," said Carmella, meaning it with all her heart.

Rose was rolling out the dough for pie crusts when her daughter entered the busy kitchen. "It smells so good in here," said Francesca, then sat down at the table.

"Mom, don't you have a job for Francesca? It doesn't seem fair she's sitting," said Mario, with humor in his voice.

"What do you think we should have her do?" asked Carmella.

"She should help me make the dressing, since you don't buy the boxes anymore. I could use some help cutting up this bread."

Rose smiled, glad that the task wasn't more difficult. She had intended to teach Francesca how to cook, but they had found other things more exciting to do, like going to the park and rollerblading and ending up at the Dairy Queen, their summer ritual on the weekends. In the winter they would go to plays and concerts. Francesca's dad, John, would go occasionally, but he preferred staying home, fixing the neighbors' cars or going fishing.

The phone rang, and everyone in the kitchen stopped what they were doing. "Hello," answered Annie. "I'm okay. Uh huh. Mr. Ryan, do you want to talk to Carmella?" Before she handed Carmella the phone, Annie whispered, "It's Mr. Ryan."

While Carmella and Henry were talking, Francesca pulled Annie to her lap and wrapped her arms around her. "How are you doing, baby girl?"

Annie giggled. "Mom, I'm not a baby anymore." She hugged her mother's arms. "I want Rudy, I mean Dad, to come home. I cleaned his room for him so it would be nice when he came home today. He had clothes on his floor. Don't get mad at him, Mom. I picked them up and put them on his dresser. I made the bed, too."

Francesca smiled. "He was sick so he didn't feel like picking up his stuff."

Annie squirmed around to look at her mother. "You're not mad, right, Mom?"

"I'm not mad, and he'll be happy you helped him out with his room."

Francesca thought about the Italian stranger who had come into her life so quickly. She had had a hard time sorting out her feelings once she had arrived back home after meeting Rudolfo—a tall, slim man with a thick Italian accent who stole her heart, and, eventually the heart of her daughter.

She loved being in New York and meeting his sister and brother-in-law and all their children, but she wanted to be alone with him. She felt there was so much more to know about this man, and she wanted to start doing things as a family. She had worked so much before their trip to New York that she hadn't been able to spend much time with them. She had to admit that she had been jealous that Annie was spending more time with Rudolfo than she was.

Every night when she had come home from work, Rudolfo and Annie had told stories about their day as they all ate dinner—a dinner prepared by the two people she loved the most. Neither one had complained of her late hours, and they had always been happy when she came home.

The phone rang again, startling her out of her thoughts. Annie jumped down from her lap and answered. "Hello. Yes, she's here, just a minute." Handing the phone to Carmella, Annie said, "It's Mr. Ryan again. Maybe he should just come over."

Carmella laughed and took the phone. "Henry, you and Sylvia come over. I'll put the coffee on." She handed the phone back to Annie.

"Thank you, Carmella."

"You're welcome, Annie. Now you better get to work and start opening those cans of vegetables. Maria will help you find everything."

*   *   *

Tony, Francesca, and Annie went to the hospital to pick up Rudolfo. When they arrived, Rudolfo was dressed and ready to go.

"Hi, Dad." Annie liked saying "Dad," and Rudolfo loved hearing it. "Are you ready to go?" She went over to the bed and took his bag, the one Tony had brought the second day Rudolfo had been in the hospital.

"Yes, I'm all checked out. I'm anxious to get home."

He sat on the bed and gave Annie a hug. "Have you been helping in the kitchen today?"

Annie shook her head. "I've never done so many chores before, and there is so much food."

He got off the bed and turned to Tony. "Carmella has probably cooked everything in the house by now."

Tony laughed. "Almost everything, and with six children she has a lot of help. You know we'll have enough food to eat for weeks to come."

"You're making me hungry," said Rudolfo. "The hospital food hasn't been very good."

"You're spoiled. Nothing tastes good unless Carmella cooks it," said Tony.

"She is a good cook," agreed Rudolfo.

Feeling left out, Francesca looked out the window while the two men continued their conversation. The sun was bright and warm, but she knew that outside it was twenty degrees. At that moment she felt very lonely. Her daughter took up a lot of Rudolfo's time and didn't seem to have much time for her. Although she was glad that Annie and Rudolfo were so close, she herself felt a void. It had started this morning with the thought of Rudolfo coming home and the house full of people who would be there to greet him.

Francesca wanted Rudolfo all to herself. How could she be alone with him, especially on Christmas, when family, so much family, should be together? She would think of something, she promised herself.

"Tony, you and Annie go bring the car around front," said Rudolfo. "I was told I have to leave in a wheelchair." He went over to the window and touched Francesca's shoulder. "Would you like to be my driver?"

She turned around and smiled at him, "Of course I would."

"Come on, Annie, let's go," said Tony.

After they left, Rudolfo said, "I didn't think I'd ever be alone with you again. I missed you."

"I was thinking the same thing. I'm glad you're feeling better. Do you feel well enough to kiss me?"

"I'm still a little weak, and if I kiss you I might get dizzy and have to stay a couple more days in the hospital." He looked at her and smiled, then put his arms around her. "But I'll take my chances," he said, and kissed her.

*　　*　　*

When the four of them entered the kitchen, Francesca noticed a different smell than when she'd left earlier. The two oldest De Luca children were at the stove. Caterina was stirring a big pot of spaghetti sauce, and Antonio was putting spaghetti noodles in boiling water.

Sensing Francesca's confusion, Tony explained. "Carmella is about as Americanized as anyone can get, but she's Italian first before anything else and she just can't help herself when it comes to Italian cooking. I've told her as long as she makes the traditional meal, she can make anything else she wants."

"I just can't imagine doing so much cooking," said Francesca.

"Me either," agreed Tony.

Rudolfo greeted each of the children. He gave his sister a kiss on the cheek and told her he was going upstairs to rest. He took Francesca's hand, and Annie started to follow. "Annie," said Carmella, "will you help me with these dishes?"

Annie looked at Rudolfo. He said, "You can help, Annie. I won't be resting for very long."

"Okay. I cleaned your room for you. I hope you like it."

"I'm sure I will."

Annie turned around and skipped to Carmella across the spacious kitchen. Rudolfo led Francesca through the living room and stopped when he noticed Rose sitting in the recliner with her feet up. "Looks like Carmella has overworked you."

"I'll say," said Rose. "Before anyone noticed, I was going to sneak upstairs and sleep for a week."

Rudolfo laughed. "You can sneak away with us."

The three of them headed for the hall and disappeared up the stairs.

*　　*　　*

Rudolfo and Francesca went to Rudolfo's room. He noticed that his clothes were no longer on the floor but folded on the dresser. His dress shoes and tennis shoes were lined up in the corner, his suitcase was sitting on the chair next to the window, and his bed was made. "I like my room this way. It's nice and neat. I'm not used to that." Rudolfo looked at Francesca. "I like you in my room, too. Lie down with me."

He had his arm around her warm body, holding her close. The back of her fit nicely to the front of his body. He kissed her on her neck. "You feel good, Francesca, but I'm too exhausted do to anything about it."

"I love you," she whispered.

He slept until he had visions of Annie and himself in a grocery store and of a woman pulling Annie into her car. Rudolfo woke with a start, felt Francesca next to him, and knew he had only been dreaming.

Francesca turned to face him. "Are you all right?" she asked, thinking he might be feeling sick again.

He knew that if he told Francesca about his dream, she would worry and it would spoil her Christmas, so he made light of the situation. "I dreamt Carmella sent us home without any food."

She laughed. "You were dreaming."

There was a knock on the door, and Carmella entered the room. "Dinner's ready," she said, adding in Italian, "Behave yourself, little brother." Then she left the room, keeping the door open.

Rudolfo helped Francesca out of bed. "I like Minnesota. No sister to boss me around." He was laughing as they left the room.

Chapter Seventeen

They went down the back stairs that Francesca hadn't known existed. Rudolfo showed her a dining room with the table set for twelve people, with a white tablecloth, white china plates, wine goblets, and crystal glasses filled with ice water.

"It looks like a table right out of Better Homes and Gardens." She looked around the room in awe. "Are we sitting in here?"

"No, we get to sit in the dining room off the kitchen."

"Then who sits in here?"

"When Carmella and Tony moved to New York they met other Italian couples, but Carmella took a special interest in the elderly couples, the ones who don't have family here and can't really afford to celebrate the holidays. Every Christmas she invites them for dinner."

"I was wondering why she was making so much food." She looked at Rudolfo, and said, "You have a wonderful sister. "

"She's rough around the edges, but she has a good heart."

They walked into the kitchen and Francesca was surprised at the clean room. The pots and pans were washed and put away; nothing was sitting out on the counters. There was no sign that anyone had been there an hour earlier cooking up a storm. The only thing left behind was the enticing aroma of a holiday meal that was about to be served.

"Francesca, before we go into the dining room, be ready for a lot of chatter, too much food, and a lot of love."

The surge of emotions that went through Francesca at that moment surprised her. She took his hand and held tight. "Stay close to me, Rudolfo. I need you right now."

"I will be right here, my love."

The main dining room was as elegant as the one they had just left, only there were more places at the table. Giovanni and Annie were putting the finishing touches on the table when Francesca and Rudolfo walked in. Giovanni was folding the cloth napkins, and Annie was placing them just right at each person's plate.

"Hi, Mom and Dad, we're almost done. We got behind because we had to go downstairs and put all the presents under the tree."

"There's a downstairs?" asked Francesca.

"Yep, it's big, too. This is the last napkin—we better get in the living room," said Annie.

The two adults followed the two children, only to be greeted with a room full of people. There were quite a few that Francesca didn't recognize. Rudolfo left her right away, went across the room, and embraced an Italian man. They kissed each other on both cheeks and conversed in Italian. Rudolfo looked at Francesca and held his hand out, and she went to him and took it.

"Francesca, this is my good friend Filipo."

Filipo embraced Francesca and kissed her on the cheek. "Ah, Rudy, she more beautiful than you describe."

"Rudolfo has told me so much about you. I'm glad you could be here for Christmas."

With a frown on his face, Rudolfo asked, "How did Carmella ever convince you to come to the United States?"

"She told me you not coming back. You get married and stay in Minnesota the rest of your life."

"In other words, she bribed you." Rudolfo laughed.

"That she did."

"How do you like the United States?"

"Too big, too crowded, too noisy. Your sister tell me to stay until wedding, but I not stay that long. I have goldfish to feed at home."

Rudolfo let out a peel of laughter. "You have no goldfish, my friend, but I am so happy you came."

Carmella came over and talked briefly, then she was off in another direction. Rudolfo's nieces and nephews were introduced to Filipo, and finally they saw Rose. Filipo kissed Rose on the cheek. "You lovely lady just like your daughter."

"Thank you," said Rose, blushing.

Carmella made the announcement that dinner was about to be served. While everyone was still standing, Tony said grace in American and Italian. Francesca asked Rose where Annie was, and Rose pointed across the room. They were able to introduce Filipo to Annie before she, Maria, and Giovanni went back to the kitchen.

Seating was not assigned, but the Italian couples knew exactly where their dining room was located. The women wore long black dresses and their husbands their worn suits of various colors. The couples were in their seventies and enjoyed the holidays at the De Lucas' home. Some of the couples didn't drive, so they weren't able to get out and visit people when they wanted. Now, this was their opportunity to see their cherished friends, given that Tony picked up the couples that didn't drive.

Chattering in Italian and laughing, they sat down. Unlike before, there was hot food on the table and the wine was already poured. The guests had a good time as they passed the food and filled each other in on their lives.

The setting in the other dining room wasn't much different. As Rudolfo had promised, there was a lot of chatter and a lot of food. Francesca was especially intrigued by Filipo. He was as tall and thin as Rudolfo, but he had short black hair and wire-rimmed glasses. His thick Italian accent, sounded just like Rudolfo's when he had arrived in Minnesota.

"Mom," asked Maria, "do we have to go to church tonight?"

It was the first time one of the children had asked if they had to do something. Francesca was interested in what Carmella would say and had her full attention on her, but Henry spoke first.

"We can watch the children, Carmella. They've been working so hard, and they have to get up early in the morning, too."

Francesca thought that getting up early meant opening Christmas presents and seeing what Santa had brought, but she would find out that that was not true.

"How many of you want to stay home with Mr. and Mrs. Ryan?" asked Tony.

All six of the De Luca children raised their hands, and then Annie's went up. "You know if you don't go tonight, you have to go tomorrow."

Antonio spoke first. "We know. Can we go to the sunrise service before we head out in the morning?"

"No, it's too early. I'll be sleeping," said Carmella, taking a sip of wine.

"I'll take them," said Tony. "Then I'll come home and sleep for an hour."

"Now that we have that settled, I'm going to check on our other guests," said Carmella, and left the room.

There were groans among the guests when Mario and Franco brought out the tray with four different kinds of pie. It was all cut; they just had to serve it on the plates that were already on the table. The pie was given out and the coffee pot was passed around. When everyone was done eating, the children got busy and cleared the table and then stayed in the kitchen until the dishes were washed, dried, and put away.

All the guests moved downstairs to a lovely decorated room. The tree was beautiful, with white and red poinsettias, colored lights, and handmade ornaments. Francesca, Rudolfo, and Filipo wandered around and talked with Tony's brothers, then moved on to the other guests.

Francesca made her way to Rose, and they were finally able to talk to each other. "What's Jerry doing for Christmas, Mom?"

"He's joining us here in the morning and then going to his son's house in the afternoon. He invited me to come to his house for New Year's Eve. I told him to come here, and he said he wasn't sure he could handle so many people at one time."

"There are a lot people here, but I'm really enjoying myself. I think Annie is, too. We lead such a sheltered life, Mom. No big holiday celebrations, not much cooking, and we don't get together with friends very often."

"When we get back home, we'll have to change that." Rose looked across the room at Rudolfo. "He looks tired, Francesca. Maybe you can convince him to go up and rest."

"I doubt if he will, but I can try." She gave her mom a hug. "Merry Christmas, Mom. I love you." Then she walked over to Rudolfo.

Rose went upstairs and used the phone in the hall to call Jerry. His guests had left and he was relaxing in front of the fire. Rose convinced him to leave the warmth of his home and spend some time with her. Jerry said he would be there in twenty minutes.

*　　*　　*

Except for the children, and Henry and Sylvia, everyone was at Our Lady of Hope for midnight mass. They filled several pews, and Rose convinced Jerry to come. Christmas carols were being sung, and Francesca was sitting with Rudolfo's arm around her, her eyes closed, enjoying the familiar songs. She suddenly realized how tired she was. Rudolfo had been able to get some sleep before church, but Francesca had stayed up and talked with Filipo. She had wanted to find out more about the man she was going to marry, and she had.

She learned that he loved painting and writing. If he could stay in his apartment all day, every day, and do those things, he would be a happy man. But most of all he loved Florence.

Filipo, though, didn't see this as a problem, not after seeing the two of them together.

Filipo told Francesca that Rudolfo was an honest man with simple dreams. He wanted to get married and have children and instill in them the importance of the history of his country, Italy.

Before they went to church, Filipo told Francesca about how nervous Rudolfo had been when she had come to the coffee shop and stepped on his foot. "He was concerned you not meet him again, Signorina, and he so happy you did."

Chapter Eighteen

The children were back from church and busy making sandwiches with leftover ham, turkey, and Italian sausage. Annie was helping Maria put the meat on top after Giovanni and Franco put mayonnaise or butter on the bread. Mario and Caterina wrapped the sandwiches and put them into baskets.

There were three pans of brownies that were cut, wrapped, and put into separate baskets. There was a basket filled with apples.

Antonio was helping his father load up the van with bottled water. "Mom is usually up by now, she must really be tired."

"If she's not up when we get back, I'll wake her up."

"You don't think she'll sleep that long, do you? She has to make caramel rolls."

Tony laughed. "No, she'll be up by then." He thought of all his son had done over the holidays to help out. Tony put his arm around him and said, "I'm very proud of you, son."

"Thanks, Dad." Antonio walked over to the van with a smile on his face. "The sooner we get done, the sooner we can open presents, right, Dad?"

"Yes, indeed, we can," said his dad with a smile on his face. They had finished loading the van when Jerry pulled up in front of the house.

* * *

The adults were watching the production line and were amazed at the dedication of each child, knowing that unopened presents were waiting for them downstairs. Once the baskets were all packed and they knew where they were going, they were eager to get started.

"Grandma, will you come with Maria and me?" Franco said to Rose.

Rose felt a warmth—the same warmth she had felt the night Franco had said he wanted her to be his grandmother. "I would love to. Can Jerry come, too?"

"Yeah, the more the better. I was looking at my presents last night, and the one sent from Annie has me confused. It shakes, but I can't figure out what it is."

"I think all the presents she bought shake," said Rose.

There was a giggle somewhere in the crowd of children and adults that Rose recognized as Annie's. "Well, we better get going so you can open it. Where are we going?"

"We are heading down the block to some neighbors' houses. One lady got sick and she has to stay in bed and her two children are too little to help around the house. In our basket we have leftovers from yesterday and sandwiches," said Franco.

Jerry helped Rose with her coat and realized that the alone time he had been expecting to have with her was not going to happen. Maybe we could get away after the presents have been opened, he thought.

Tony was driving Antonio and Giovanni to the church shelter. "Filipo, will you drive Caterina, Mario, and Annie downtown?"

"No, no, me no drive!"

"I guess I remember that now. Francesca, will you drive? One of them has the directions."

"Sure, I'll drive."

Filipo decided he would go with Francesca, as he wanted to get to know the woman his best friend would marry. The night before he had answered a lot of questions about Rudolfo, but today he had questions of his own.

Rudolfo and Carmella were still asleep when the last team left. The house was still, with no activity, no cooking or chatter. It seemed that the house, too, needed a break from the commotion that had been so apparent the several days before Christmas. Soon, however, the aroma of caramel rolls would fill the air, the chatter would return, and the activity would be focused on the lower level of the house while the presents were opened.

*　　*　　*

On the way home all of the children were quiet, reflecting on the mission their mother sent them on every year. The urgency to open presents was lessened as they realized there were people who could not afford gifts.

When they got home, Francesca took Annie upstairs to talk to her, as she could tell that her daughter had been saddened by their outing.

"Mom, do they really sleep outside?" asked Annie, trying not to cry.

"Yes, they do." Francesca explained as best she could without getting her daughter more upset.

"Do they sleep outside in Minnesota?"

"Yes."

"Next Christmas, Mom, we should make them sandwiches," suggested Annie, wiping her eyes. She hugged her mom and after a few minutes wanted to go back downstairs. Francesca lay down on the bed, and exhaustion washed over her. As her eyes were about to close, Rudolfo knocked gently on the door and walked in.

"Are you okay?" asked Rudolfo. He sat down on the bed and stroked Francesca's hair. "I know the first time I went out on Christmas morning I felt sad for days."

"I'm okay. I'm worried about Annie, though."

"She's downstairs eating. I think she'll be okay."

Rudolfo knelt and kissed her forehead; then his lips lingered as he moved down her face and found her lips. He kissed her neck and let out a groan. "Signorina, Ti amo."

"I love you, too."

The sexual tension had been building since Rudolfo had gotten out of the hospital. It was hard for the two even to talk to each other with all the people in the house, but they longed to be alone, to be in each other's arms.

He opened the top button on her blouse, and then his lips moved down her neck. "You make me mad, Francesca." His arms went under her neck and he kissed her passionately, inching his body onto hers. This time Francesca let out a groan.

"Fratello piccolo, alimento in cucina, pensi al signorina, sono offenduto." Carmella threw up her arms, let out a wicked laugh, and left.

Rudolfo buried his head in the pillow and laughed uncontrollably. Francesca smiled, watching him. "What did she say?"

He tried hard not to laugh while telling Francesca what his sister had said. "She said, 'My little brother . . . you know there is food downstairs and all you can think of . . . is your signorina. I'm offended.'" They both laughed and fell back on the bed.

*   *   *

The caramel rolls were devoured, and everyone was seated downstairs. Jerry was able to stay before he went to his son's house for dinner later in the afternoon. He didn't want to admit it, but he was enjoying the children, especially Annie. Once she had called him Grandpa, and he had just smiled at her.

Jerry hadn't been with a woman in a long time, and after being with Rose he regretted the wasted years. There was only one problem that he could see with their relationship—the miles between them. He couldn't leave his family, and Rose wouldn't leave hers.

*   *   *

The two older children passed out the presents, and when they were all distributed the adults opened theirs first. The youngest children were last, and Giovanni could hardly wait to open the present he got from Annie. He kept it in his lap while he sat on the floor next to Annie, and she had in her hands the present that Giovanni had given her.

Annie leaned over and whispered in his ear, "Giovanni, let's go over there behind the chairs and you can open your present."

"Mom would be mad, but let's go. I'll go first and then you come." He crawled off and seconds later Annie followed.

No one noticed them as they leaned against the backs of the adults' chairs. "You open yours first," said Annie.

He carefully unwrapped the paper, opened the box, took off the tissue paper, and took out the wooden cylinder kaleidoscope. He held it up to his eye and twisted it around. "Annie, this is so cool." He passed it to her to look.

She was already familiar with it, but she liked to look at the multicolored crystals twirling around and the butterflies that appeared. Annie gave it back, and Giovanni looked again. He put it back in the box and closed the lid. "I like my present. Thank you, Annie."

"It's small enough to fit in your pocket so you can take it with you all the time."

She picked up the small package that Giovanni had wrapped for her and opened it. She took the cotton out of the box and found a yellow fire truck pin. "Hey," she whispered, "this is so nice." She took off the back, put the pin through her red sweater, and pushed the back on securely. "How does it look?"

"It looks nice. Do you really like it?"

"Yeah, it will remind me of when we went to the fire station." She rubbed her hand on it and smiled. "Should we sneak back now?" Then they heard their names being called.

They crawled back out, Giovanni being extra careful so as to not break the kaleidoscope. "What have you two been up to?" asked Carmella.

"Um, we were . . ."

"Come here, you two." She took them in her arms and kissed them both. "Now show us your presents."

Francesca watched while they explained their gifts and showed everyone what they had received. She knew that her daughter was having a great time and dreaded the day they had to go back home, but once she and Rudolfo were married they would visit the De Luca family regularly. And the De Lucas could visit Minnesota.

Carmella winked at Rudolfo. He took his cue and announced that he and Francesca were walking to the coffee shop down the block. When Annie and Giovanni wanted to come along, Carmella told them that only adults were invited, and Filipo offered to help them play with their toys. Maria giggled and said, "You want to play with my doll?"

Rose asked how big the coffee shop was and suggested that she and Jerry go along—they would get their own table. When it was decided that the four of them would go, they put on their coats and started the trek down the block. Both couples were arm in arm and enjoying the quiet, the sun, and the cool afternoon air.

*   *   *

Christmas songs were playing in the café, and several families were enjoying the warm drinks. The lady at the counter, was short and thin, and had a wide smile on her face.

"Welcome to our home for the holidays. We don't have family"—she pointed to her husband—"so we stay open while people come and visit us."

Her husband joined her at the counter. "What can we get for you all?"

*   *   *

"Francesca, I thought I'd never be alone with you." Rudolfo pulled a box from his coat pocket and handed it to her. "Merry Christmas."

She looked at him. "Thank you."

"You haven't opened it yet."

"Anything from you is special." She unwrapped the paper and then opened the box. "Oh! This is so beautiful." She held out the necklace so Rudolfo could put it on her. She turned in her chair, and he fumbled with the clasp. "The green stones match the ones in my ring."

When the necklace was on, she turned to face Rudolfo. "I just love it."

"I'm glad, but I have to admit I had help selecting the right one."

"Annie?"

"Yes, she was so excited helping me."

Francesca took Rudolfo's present out of her bag and handed it to him. "It's a little early to be giving you this, but I wanted you to see it anyway."

He took the lid off the box and took out the silver wedding band. There was a hint of green, inlaid throughout the band. With tears in his eyes Rudolfo kissed Francesca and thanked her. "Can I wear it now?"

"You can see if it fits."

He put it on and it fit perfectly. "It looks good on. I'm going to keep wearing it."

"I don't know if that's such a good idea. There might be some kind of bad luck that will happen if you are wearing it before we get married."

"No, bad luck, Francesca. Being with you is all good. I will wear it and when we get married it will be even more special to me." He kissed her again. "When should we get married? I don't want to wait much longer."

"I don't either. Once we get back to Minnesota we can decide on a date." She had a sad look on her face.

"What's the matter, Signorina?"

She took his hand. "You live so far away, and we haven't even talked about where we will live and if you'll want to leave Florence."

"Let's wait until we get back to Minnesota before we talk about such serious things. I want to enjoy each minute with you and I want them to be happy. Now don't look so sad, my love." He took her other hand. "Now you kiss me, no?"

*　　*　　*

Jerry slid an envelope across the table to Rose. "I wasn't going to get you a present, but I decided you need this more than anything. Or I should say I need this more than anything."

She took the envelope and opened it. There was one round-trip plane ticket to New York for the end of January. She looked at Jerry.

"I realized after you came that I've missed out on so much by working so hard and not taking time out for myself. I don't think I can make it more than a month without seeing you again. You don't have to use it if you don't want to."

"Jerry . . ."

"I would understand if you never wanted to come back to New York."

"Jerry . . ."

"So if you say no, I'll just move on with my life and forget we saw each other."

"Hush." Rose moved closer to him "Listen to me. I will use the tickets. Then in February you come to Minnesota."

The confusion on his face turned to a smile, and he leaned over to her and kissed her. "If I didn't have to leave soon you'd be at my home sitting by the fire and I would be tasting your sweet kisses." Rose blushed. "Can I call you tonight?"

"Yes, call me," said Rose.

Chapter Nineteen

The rest of Christmas day was for relaxing. The younger children played with their toys and the older ones downloaded their new programs on the computer. Rudolfo was tired and went upstairs to lay down.

He thought about Francesca bringing up whether or not he wanted to leave Florence. He wanted to live in Florence and had never thought he would move away from Italy. Annie was doing well with her Italian—she might be a little slow in school at first, but she was young and would be a fast learner. Francesca came to Florence all the time anyway and thought she knew enough Italian to get around the city, and he thought if she lived there she could make frequent trips back to America instead. Rose could also travel to Florence to be with her family.

He knew he was being unreasonable and probably even selfish, but he loved Italy and didn't think he could live anywhere else. Next week when they were back in Minnesota he would try to convince Francesca to move.

*   *   *

Jerry and Rose saw each other every day. Annie enjoyed playing with the De Luca children. Francesca and Rudolfo walked to the coffee shop every morning and had coffee and scones. Tony was on call at work and had to go in several times to help with the computer system. Carmella, if she ever took off her robe, would go to the grocery store. She told her family it was her week for rest and relaxation. Although she was a hard worker, she also knew how to take it easy and let her family wait on her.

*   *   *

"I will be going to Jerry's house for New Year's Eve," Rose announced at the dinner table. "He wants to know if anyone wants to join him at his house to watch videos and play games."

Annie raised her hand, "I do, Grandma."

"We don't usually do anything on that day anyway, so it would be nice to get away," said Carmella.

With a grin on his face, Antonio said, "Mom, you'll have to change out of that robe and put on real clothes."

"Well, if one of you had gotten me one of those nice fluffy robes for Christmas, I wouldn't have to change out of this tattered one."

Tony laughed, as did the children. "You know full well we were warned not to replace it."

Carmella smiled and looked at Rose. "Yes, tell Jerry we will all come."

*   *   *

Carmella made most of the food; even though her week for relaxing was not yet up, she welcomed getting dressed, cooking, and getting things ready for the New Year celebration, which meant that the children were assigned duties. Caterina commented, "Mom, you should relax more, take it easy. We can buy some food. We don't eat that much anyway."

Carmella laughed and hugged her daughter. "My beautiful child, do I really work you that hard?"

"Yes, Momma, you do."

"Why don't you go find Annie and Giovanni and take them to Henry's? He should be making his famous biscuits by now. Maybe he'll give you some."

Caterina's face brightened. "Thanks, Momma! What time do you want us back?"

"I'll call you when we're ready. Invite Sylvia and Henry over tomorrow for New Year's."

She brushed her daughter's hair away from her face. "Dress warm."

*   *   *

Rose helped Jerry get his house organized, found the videos and placed them by the TV, and got the games set up on several tables. They were both relieved when Carmella told them not to worry; she would provide all the food. They did wonder if they should serve such fine food on paper plates or get out the dishes. They decided on paper plates, and Jerry went to the store and bought those as well as plastic ware. Rose stayed and curled up on the couch in front of the fireplace. Soon she was asleep.

*   *   *

Francesca knocked on Rudolfo's door. "Come in."

When she sat next to him on the bed, he sat up. "What's troubling you, Francesca?"

"I don't think I can wait to find out where we will live and when we will get married." She looked down at her hands. "I want to find out now what your thoughts are about us."

He took her hands. "We can marry whenever you want to set the date."

"I want to get married in May. Will you be able to come to Minnesota then?"

He knew the next question to be settled after the wedding date would be where they would live. He still didn't want to leave Florence, but if he told Francesca that now, it would ruin the rest of their time in New York. "May will be a lovely time of year for a wedding. I would like my sister to be there." Trying to avoid the dreaded question that he knew would follow, he added, "Let's go down and ask Carmella if it's a good time to get away."

Rudolfo got off the bed and pulled Francesca into him. "I have such inner turmoil that I don't think I can discuss where we will live right now. I hope you can understand that."

"I'm having the same problem", said Francesca. "Okay, let's talk about it when we get home." She looked into his eyes. "Now you kiss me, yes?"

"Yes." He pulled her closer and kissed her. "Let's lock the door and make love, yes?"

"No! We should go downstairs and talk to Carmella and Tony. I want to call Mom, too, about the date. Let's have it on the second Saturday in May."

He kissed her again. He wanted her—there was no doubt about that in the way he kissed her.

*   *   *

Jerry knelt down by Rose on the couch and kissed her on her cheek and neck, then rested his lips on hers until she was aroused and woke up. "I hated to wake you up, but our guests will be arriving soon."

She pulled him to her and they kissed again. He put his arms around her and inched his body onto hers, then kissed her deeply, passionately. The doorbell rang, but he didn't hear it. Rose tried to move but he was focused on one thing. Her! The door opened and Francesca yelled, "Mom, are you here?"

Jerry quickly got off the couch and pulled Rose with him. She combed her fingers through her hair in an attempt to look presentable, and then they both went into the kitchen.

"Grandma, your hair is messy—were you sleeping?"

Rudolfo and Francesca realized they had interrupted more than just sleep. Francesca felt awkward and didn't know what to say.

"Yes," said Jerry, "she was sleeping, and it took me a while to wake her up." He looked at Rudolfo and saw the grin on his face. "Is everyone here?"

"No, we decided to come early to help."

"Sorry we woke you up, Grandma," said Annie. "I'm good at doing chores, so tell me what you want me to do."

Rose handed Annie the grocery bag from Jerry's shopping trip. "I'm not sure where to put these—arrange them on the kitchen table or just leave them on the cupboard."

"I'll take care of it, Grandma."

Jerry didn't think he could last until after midnight when everyone left to have Rose all to himself again. She was going home in two days and he wanted to be alone with her as much as he could. He would get through the night, he told himself, and hopefully Rose would spend the night with him.

*   *   *

The children were having fun playing games and Jerry's family blended in well with everyone. The adults opted to sit in the living room and talk. Filipo was going home tomorrow, and he was enjoying his friend's family and, of course, Francesca and her family. He wasn't able to be alone with Francesca much, but from what he had observed, Francesca was not like the other women Rudolfo dated. Filipo thought he might even come back for the wedding.

*   *   *

Jerry turned on the TV ten minutes before midnight. The effects of Dick Clark's stroke several years back were obvious in his speech, but he had a smile on his face and seemed just as happy as in years past. When the ball dropped, the children jumped up and down yelling "Happy New Year!"

The adults embraced and kissed. Annie and Giovanni hugged each other, then went to the other children and did the same thing. Thirty minutes later, the women had the kitchen cleaned and the food packed up, and the children were getting their coats on.

Everyone thanked Jerry for a nice party, and when they all left, Rose and Jerry sat by the fire with their feet propped up. "I had fun. Did you?" asked Jerry.

"I had a lot of fun."

Jerry stood, took Rose's hand, and helped her up. "Let's continue the fun. Follow me."

Chapter Twenty

Annie and Francesca sat together on the plane back to Minnesota. Rose and Rudolfo sat in the seats in front of them. Rudolfo was thinking about going back to Italy after he had spent a few more days with Francesca. He had been able to talk to Filipo before he went back home. Filipo told Rudolfo he needed to make his own decision on where to live, but he did advise his friend to look into dual citizenship.

Rose was thinking about New Year's morning when she woke up in Jerry's arms. They felt that seeing each other once a month would not be enough unless the visits were for two weeks at a time. Rose felt saddened that they were going back home. There were so many good memories about New York—not just for her and Jerry, but for Annie. For all her grandchildren, she reminded herself, as the De Luca children had adopted her early in her visit.

Annie had the tray table down in front of her while she wrote to Giovanni, but mostly she drew pictures. After she finished that letter she was going to write to Maria. Francesca had told her she could mail the letters at the airport once they landed. She took her notebook out of her backpack and opened to the page with the New York address and all the children's names.

She even had Sylvia and Henry's address. She would write to them after she got home and unpacked.

Annie didn't know what she would do at home without someone to play with all the time, and Carmella had certainly kept her busy. She would have to ask her mom to make up a chores list for her to do every day. Rudolfo had told her he was going home soon. She had felt like crying thinking he would never come back, but he had promised he would.

Francesca thought about the strong family ties between Rudolfo and his sister. The children loved their uncle and many times asked him questions about school and everyday life. Would he consider moving to New York instead of Minnesota? Francesca thought she could handle that better than she could moving to Florence.

Carmella had suggested June for the wedding because the children would be out of school then, but had said whatever was decided on would work. So Francesca and Rudolfo decided on a June wedding, and with Rudolfo at his home in Florence, Rose would be the only one who could help with the wedding preparations.

Among all the good memories and thoughts of the upcoming wedding, Francesca kept thinking about Annie's safety. She hoped that the woman who had followed Annie would've given up by now, but she couldn't take that risk. Annie could never be left alone outside or walk to the store until this was cleared up. Her daughter might have to be told what had happened so that she would understand the concern.

She looked over at her daughter and smiled. "I love you, Annie."

Annie looked up. "I love you, too, Mom," she said, and then continued writing.

*   *   *

Rose went home after they arrived at Francesca's house, and Annie was tucked in and sleeping. Both exhausted from the trip, Rudolfo and Francesca kissed each other goodnight and went to their separate bedrooms.

Sleep did not come easily for Rudolfo. Most of all, Annie, was on his mind. What if the woman came back? Would Annie ever be able to go anywhere on her own without supervision? Then his thoughts would drift to the wedding, where they would live, how Annie would adjust to the schools in Italy. And what about Rose? Would she be able to cope with her only child and grandchild living in Italy? She wouldn't be able to just get in the car and visit the way she did now.

He needed to talk to Filipo. They hadn't had much of an opportunity to talk in New York, but Rudolfo really needed him now. Deciding to call him, he went back upstairs and used the phone in the kitchen.

It America it was early in the morning, but when no one answered, Rudolfo suspected that Filipo was already out and having his cup of coffee and sandwich at the corner café, the one where they so often met. Rudolfo missed home and wanted to be drinking coffee with his friend. He had a lot to think about, and it looked as though he would have to figure things out on his own.

*   *   *

Early the next morning, before Annie was up, Rudolfo and Francesca took their coffee downstairs to talk.

Francesca said, "I haven't asked Annie where she wants to live." She took a sip of coffee. "The wedding will take place after she gets out of school, but where do we live after that?"

Without consulting his friend and not thinking rationally, Rudolfo said, "I want to live in Florence." He put his cup down. "Most of the people speak English, as you know from traveling there so often." He stared into Francesca's troubled blue eyes.

It took several minutes for Francesca to comprehend what Rudolfo was saying. He wants to stay in Italy. Annie and I will be someplace where we don't know anyone. We would have to travel all the way back to Minnesota to see my mother. What if I lost my job?—a job I love. Annie will be lonely if she can't see her friends on a regular basis, especially Grace.

Rudolfo would be leaving only Filipo. Yes, Filipo is his best friend, she thought, but he could come to the States. He said he enjoyed America.

Francesca was still tired from traveling, and now she had to make a life-changing decision. It was more than she could handle right now. The only reason she would move to Florence would be if Annie was in danger because of the woman following her.

"Francesca?" He took her hand. "What are you thinking?"

"I can't think. It's all too much right now. Had I thought of the reality of this whole thing ahead of time, I would never have allowed myself to fall in love with you."

She stood and walked up the stairs, leaving Rudolfo stunned by her words. He had thought that she might need time to think about moving and that they could work something out, but he was not prepared for what she had just said.

He ran up the stairs to the kitchen, but she wasn't there. Then he went down the hall. Her bedroom door was closed. It made him angry that now she had closed herself off from him. He went back to the kitchen, put on his coat and gloves, then went outside and headed down the sidewalk.

He loved Francesca with all his being, and he anguished over the idea that he might lose her because of his selfishness. Maybe they needed to be apart for a while to sort things out. He put his gloved hands over his ears. Damn weather, I could never adjust to this cold.

He was going home tomorrow, but first he had to get Francesca to talk to him and try to convince her to trust him. All of a sudden he lost his footing and his body slammed against the iced cement. Pain shot through his elbow. "Damn this weather to hell!!" Carefully, Rudolfo stood, brushed himself off, and instead of going back to the house, kept walking until he came to the corner store and went in.

Annie had shown him the back room of the store where the owner sold coffee and scones. Now, Rudolfo went back, sat down, and within minutes the owner poured him coffee and brought him an apricot scone, the kind he and Annie always ordered.

"Good morning, sir, how was your Christmas in New York?"

"We all had a good time, thank you."

"You'll probably be going home soon. I know that little girl will miss you."

"I'll miss her, too."

The owner touched Rudolfo's coat. "It's ripped. You didn't fall, did you? It's slippery out there—be careful."

Without commenting further, the owner went back behind the counter. Rudolfo was glad, since he was embarrassed that he had fallen. He sipped his coffee and when he'd finished his scone he thought it just wasn't the same without Annie to keep him company. Maybe he could adjust to living here. Annie was a good companion when Francesca was at work. But he told himself he would never adjust to the cold.

*   *   *

Annie and Francesca were at the kitchen table, Francesca drinking coffee and Annie eating her breakfast, when Rudolfo came through the door.

"Hi, Rudy," said Annie. She got down and went to him. "Hey, did you go get coffee and a scone without me?"

"How would you know if I did?" asked Rudolfo, irritated that she knew.

"Because you smell like coffee! I thought we made a pact we wouldn't go without each other." She had a sad look on her face.

Francesca went over to them. "Annie, I got angry at Rudolfo, and he left and went for coffee."

"How could you, Mom!" Annie put her arms around Rudolfo's leg and looked at her mom. "Do you need to apologize?"

Francesca laughed. "I'm not sure. It might be something the three of us have to talk about."

"Then we better talk about it right now," said Annie.

Rudolfo took off his coat and joined them at the table. "Rudy, your shirt is ripped and you're bleeding."

He looked at the hole in his shirt and his bloody elbow. It still hurt from the fall, but he didn't think he was bleeding.

"Let's go to the bathroom and I'll clean it for you," said Francesca. "What happened?"

Rudolfo followed Francesca into the bathroom with Annie trailing behind. "I fell." As he remembered the fall, the pain got worse. He took off his shirt, and the only one bothered by his naked chest was Francesca. Even though she was upset at him, she found it hard to concentrate while she washed his wound. Rudolfo grimaced from the pain. "I'm sorry. I'm done now. I'll bandage it."

Luckily Rudolfo and Annie were chatting, and no one noticed that her hands were unsteady from the chemistry between them.

"I think we should talk about a few things before I leave tomorrow," said Rudolfo. "Do you have any pain medicine?"

"Let's do it now, so Mom is not mad at you anymore," Annie offered.

Once they were all seated back in the kitchen, Rudolfo took something for the pain. Rudolfo told Annie how he felt about where they should live. Francesca said that she wanted to stay in Minnesota.

Annie put her elbows on the table, with her head resting in her hands, as she listened to both sides of the story. Not comprehending how far away Italy was, Annie suggested that they move halfway in between, to New York.

"Then Grace could visit me during the summer and I would be by all my cousins, and your friend Filipo could visit, too."

"It sounds logical," said Rudolfo.

Francesca agreed. "Our company has their corporate office in New York."

They all agreed to think about it until the wedding while Rudolfo was back in Italy.

Rudolfo wasn't sure how to tell Annie about what had happened, but he knew he had to tell her, and now would be the best time to do it. "Your Mom and I haven't talked about telling you this, but…" He looked at Francesca and then back at Annie. "I think you should know." Rudolfo then explained to Annie about the woman following her.

"The woman that was reading all those labels?"

"Yes."

"As long as you and Mom are with me, I'm okay, right?"

"Come here, Annie." Annie went to her mother and sat in her lap. "You're going to be okay, but don't go outside without one of us."

"I'm scared, Mom." Francesca held her daughter close to her.

"We won't let anything happen to you."

It took several more minutes to convince Annie that she was safe with them. "Can I call Grace?" Annie said. "I'll use the phone in your bedroom if it's okay, Mom."

"Sure, it's okay. Just give me another hug."

*   *   *

"Francesca, your comment about loving me hurt me deeply." Rudolfo wanted her to love him and never have any regrets. "Do you love me?"

"Yes, I do. You know I do." She looked into his sad eyes. "I was so tired from traveling and being away from home for so long that I wasn't thinking straight. I know we can work something out."

"I like Annie's idea. That way Rose will be closer to Jerry, if she decides to move with us."

A smile came to Francesca's face. "I think it's a great idea for us to move to New York," she said.

She went over to him, sat in his lap, and kissed him. "I want you, Francesca," he said. He touched her hair. "I want something to remember when I go back to Italy. I want to see your beauty in my dreams."

Desire surged through both of them. "Annie? Maybe she would like to go to Grace's house. I'll go ask her."

Minutes later Annie was ready to go to Grace's house. Francesca drove her to make sure she arrived safely, and told her that she shouldn't go anywhere unless Grace's parents were with her. Annie promised.

Chapter Twenty-One

Rudolfo was waiting anxiously for Francesca to return. He didn't know if they should make love in his bed or Francesca's. He decided to take a shower and then remembered his bandage, so he went back upstairs and paced instead until Francesca came home.

He took the wine she was carrying from her hands and placed it on the counter, along with her keys and purse. "I can't wait, my love." He kissed her feverishly, and as he moved his lips down her neck, the kisses became hotter and hotter. He removed her coat, and it fell to the floor. Then he started unbuttoning her blouse

"God, I want you. Undress for me, my sweet, sweet, love."

"Here?"

"Let's go to my room." He took her hand and led the way down the stairs to his bedroom. She undressed. "Sit in the chair—I want to sketch you first."

"Rudol . . . fo, I can't wait that long."

"Please, it won't take long." He undressed. There was an inherent strength in his face as he focused on his drawing. He drew her swollen breasts. He continued down her body and sketched her perfectly formed legs. This time he added her birthmark. Adding her eyes, her oval face, and her hair resulted in a sensuous depiction of Francesca and how he was feeling about her.

She watched his firm, beautifully proportioned body as he bent down, took blue chalk, and added it to her eyes. Each time he bent down, her feelings for him intensified. Her pulse was hammering in her ears as she moved her eyes down his body and she could see that he was just as turned on as she was. Rudolfo was capturing her passion as her dormant sexuality became fully awakened, waiting for him to finish.

Rudolfo went to her after he added the finishing touches, then pulled Francesca into his arms. His slow, drugging kisses made her weak, and his hot flesh on her body filled her whole being with wanting.

He eased her down onto the bed and kissed every inch of her. His kisses were hot and sensuous, and she couldn't bear it any longer. "Rudolfo! Now! I can't wait."

Rudolfo gently lowered his body on hers, and his gentle massage sent currents of desire through her. His body was shaking as they became one with each other, and then he couldn't get enough of her. He kept up his resolve, and even after the intensity became too much for him, he continued. Francesca was beautiful as he watched his lovely Signorina arch her back, and then it happened, their love exploded into each other.

Rudolfo moved next to her and held her close. "I love you," he said, out of breath.

"I love you, too." She wanted him to stay another day, another week, forever.

"Now, I'll have sweet dreams when I get back home."

"I will, too."

He caressed her hair and longed never to be apart from her. He wanted her to come to Italy with him when he went home and never to leave his side. "Oh, my love, never leave me. I couldn't bear it."

"Never," she said. "I will always be with you."

Rudolfo knew he had to get ready for traveling, but he pulled the woman he loved closer to him, and took much pleasure in her closeness.

The phone rang, but neither of them wanted to move away from each other. After the fourth ring, Rudolfo, said, "Stay here, I'll answer it." When he came back he told Francesca that Grace was going to her aunt's house for dinner and that Annie had to come home. Grace's parents would bring Annie home on their way.

"I'd better get dressed."

"No, not yet, I'm coming back to bed." He moved under the covers. "One more time, my love."

*   *   *

Annie and Francesca were playing cards in the living room while Rudolfo was in the kitchen talking on the phone.

"My flight leaves tomorrow at four. Is there any way I can reschedule?" He got the confirmation he needed, and was scheduled to fly home five days later. He would be alone with Francesca while Annie was in school.

Then he dialed Filipo's number. "Pronto."

"Ah, my friend, you are home. I'm getting married in June. I want you to be my best man."

"In Minnesota or New York?"

"Minnesota."

"Is it cold in June?"

"No, it's warm. I think . . ." He touched his elbow. "I hope it is."

"I come if it's warm."

"I'm staying five more days, so don't pick me up tomorrow."

He heard laughter on the line. "Then you call again and want five more days."

That made Rudolfo laugh. "Have you been to the bank with my checks as they come in the mail?"

"Yes, you give me permission to open your mail. I feel like I'm doing something wrong, no?"

"No, my friend, you are helping me out."

"Oh, Rudy, today you got a letter in the mail. It's has a woman's handwriting."

"Who is it from?"

"There's no return address."

"Would you open it?"

"That's personal. I don't open personal letters. I might get arrested."

"I'm giving you my permission. Open it and read it to me." He could hear the letter being opened. Filipo read:

My Dearest Rudolfo,

You thought you could fool me, didn't you? I saw you in New York with an American woman. You were there for over a week. She must live there. But I've seen you other places, too, so I'm not sure where she lives. Call me. I've written my phone number and address below. Let me know and I will meet you. I can take a cab anywhere you want.

Are you planning on getting married? She doesn't seem your type. Maybe I can change your mind and we can get back together.

Love, Tina

"Tear it up, Filipo!" Calming himself , he continued, "I never want to see her again."

"I just threw it in the fireplace."

Thinking that would resolve the issue, Rudolfo sighed, "Thank you, my friend."

"I thought she left Italy, because she met someone in New York and got married," said Filipo.

Every time Rudolfo recalled being left at the altar, he would feel the pain all over again. This time it didn't matter what had happened in the past. He loved Francesca now, and he would never give that up, not for anybody, especially for Tina—someone who had already broken his heart.

"I thought so, too. Is that letter destroyed yet?"

"Yes, all burned."

"I better go. Thank you, my friend, for all your help. Arrivederci."

He hung up and looked around the kitchen, noticing the bright sun reflecting off the cream-colored wallpaper. It is so bright, he thought. He wanted to go home but realized how dark his own apartment was. The walls needed painting, and the windows were slanted in a way that made it hard for the sun to shine through. The carpet was worn, but it was his home and he felt comfortable there. He would have to wait five more days to get home and then see if he could part with the apartment he had so long called home.

Rudolfo tried to calm himself before he talked to Francesca, but he just couldn't understand why the letter was sent, and why Tina wanted to get back with him again. He had no intention of ever leaving his beloved family, the one waiting for him in the next room.

"Rudy?" Startled, Rudolfo looked at Annie. "I'm hungry," she said.

"I don't remember seeing any food in the refrigerator the last time I looked."

"Can we get some food? I can stay home where it's safe."

He stood up, took Annie's hand, and went to talk to Francesca.

"Let's go out to eat—then we can go to the store and get food for tomorrow," suggested Rudolfo. He was thinking that with both of them along, they could protect Annie.

Annie had tears in her eyes. "I have to go back to school tomorrow, don't I?" she said, looking at Rudolfo with her watery blue eyes. "I won't get to take you to the airport with Mommy."

"Let's go eat and then we'll talk about it."

Annie convinced them to go to the burger place and told them that her grandmother should come, too.

*　　*　　*

After they ordered, Annie wanted to talk about school.

"I'll come and pick you up from school," said Rose, "while your mom is at the airport."

Rudolfo could see that Annie was ready to cry again, so he took her hand and said, "I've decided to stay until Saturday so you can come to the airport with us." Annie gave him a high five.

"Thanks, Dad."

Francesca was silent and filled with joy that Rudolfo was staying longer. She was thinking of all the time they would have together while Annie was in school.

Rose talked about Jerry. "He wants to come to Minnesota before I go back to New York." She looked at Francesca. "He wants to be invited to your wedding."

"Will he be my grandpa soon?" asked Annie while she colored her placemat.

"I don't know, he lives so far away."

"Mommy loves Rudy, Grandma, and he lives in Italy, and they're getting married and New York's not that far away."

"You're right, but we haven't even talked about marriage."

The waiter brought the food, and while they were eating, Rose watched her daughter look at Rudolfo. Annie talked about her new cousins and said she was excited about getting letters back from them. When they were finished eating, Francesca and Rose went to the restroom.

"You and Rudolfo made love, didn't you?"

She looked at her mother and smiled. "What do you mean?"

"You know what I mean. I can tell by the way you look at each other."

"We're always looking at each other."

"Is he a good lover?"

"Mother!"

"Well, is he?"

"Okay, I can see you aren't going to give up. Yes, we made love. No, he's not a good lover." She paused. "He's exceptional." They both laughed.

"What about you, Mom?"

"What do you mean?"

"Okay, come clean. I think you told me that if a man was kind and gentle he would be good lover. Jerry fits that profile."

"You're right. He does fit that profile." Rose blushed. "That's all I'm saying. We better get back before they wonder where we are."

When the bill was paid, Rose said she would stop by the house later, and Rudolfo, Francesca, and Annie went to the grocery store.

* * *

Annie tugged on Rudolfo's pant leg. Rudolfo bent down, and Annie said, "That woman is here." His stomach tightened and fists clenched. He didn't want to cause a scene, he just wanted Annie safe.

"Where did you see her?"

"In the last aisle we were in. She has on a brown coat."

"Francesca, we're checking out and leaving." He picked up Annie, and Francesca pushed the cart to the checkout.

Annie whispered in Rudolfo's ear, "She's looking at me—let's hurry and go home."

Without looking back, Rudolfo said, "We will and you'll be safe."

When the groceries were paid for, they proceeded to the car and drove home. Minutes later a car—the same car that Rudolfo had seen from the window weeks before—was out front. This time Rudolfo didn't hesitate to call the police. Twenty minutes later, two squad cars pulled up and questioned the woman in the car. One policeman took her away and another came to the door.

Rudolfo explained what had just happened, and what had happened before. He told the policeman that he wanted to press charges.

"You'll have to come down to the station and fill out a report," said the officer. He handed Rudolfo a business card. "The sooner the better."

*   *   *

"You're safe now, Annie," said Francesca.

"I'm still scared. What will the police do to the woman?"

"Rudolfo is going to the station to fill out a report, and then she won't be able to bother you anymore."

Rudolfo went to the station with the officer. When Rose arrived at their home, Annie had already calmed down.

Now at the station, Rudolfo explained to the policeman on duty in detail what had happened. Then he was asked to describe the incident that had occurred before they had gone to New York. The policeman wrote everything down.

"Do you want to press charges?"

"Yes, I do."

"After you find out who it is, you might change your mind."

"What do you mean?"

"She says she knows you."

"I don't know anyone in Minnesota."

"She claims you knew each other in Italy." Rudolfo stiffened in his chair. "Her name is Tina Moretti," said the officer.

He thought of the letter Filipo read to him over the phone and felt anger rising through his body. "Where is she?" he asked.

"She's being questioned."

Rudolfo looked through the glass window and saw police officers at their desks doing paperwork or talking to coworkers. He scanned the space until he spotted her sitting at a desk on the far side of the room. He stood up.

"Sit down—I have more questions to ask you," the policeman said.

Rudolfo ignored him and walked slowly but deliberately to the desk where Tina was sitting as the policeman followed close behind him. When she saw him she said, "Hi, Rudolfo, how are you?"

She had changed. Her long black hair was now light brown and short, and she had put on weight since the last time Rudolfo had seen her. He chided himself for not recognizing her, and then maybe, he told himself, this would've been stopped right from the start.

He raised his voice and shouted at her in Italian. "I never did anything to you but stupidly fall in love with you. Why are you stalking us? Don't you have your own life? After you left me at the altar, you told me in your letter that you loved someone else. You leave that little girl alone or I'll make sure you're not alive to do it again."

Tina had been sitting there with a smile on her face. As she listened to what Rudolfo had to say, the smile disappeared. She had never seen him so angry. She hesitated, then looked at the officer and said, "He just threatened me!"

"You'd better calm down, sir, or I'll have you arrested."

"I want to press charges and I want a restraining order against her."

"What are you pressing charges for?" asked Tina.

He glared at her as anger consumed his body, then quickly turned away and talked directly to the officer. "I'm ready to fill out the report."

"Wait a minute. You just threatened her."

"I did not, and it's my word against hers, unless you know Italian. Besides, who are you going to believe, me or someone who stalks little girls?"

Tina looked shocked and was about to say something but decided against it.

"All right, come to my office, but one more outburst and I'll lock you up."

When both reports were filled out, Rudolfo left with a copy of the restraining order and was told he would be notified of Tina's court date for sentencing. He was given a ride back home from an officer just getting off duty.

Could he leave Minnesota now? He wanted to be there for court. He would probably have to cancel his flight and call his editor. He was scheduled to illustrate several children's books and hoped he would have time once he got back home—but when would he get back home?

Chapter Twenty–Two

When Rudolfo came through the door, Annie ran to him and he hugged her. "Am I safe now?"

"Yes, you're safe."

Rudolfo told them that he had pressed charges and filled out a restraining order against the woman, and that Annie would be safe.

He didn't tell them that he knew the stalker. He would tell Francesca and Rose after Annie went to bed.

*   *   *

Rudolfo retold the story and this time left nothing out. "I'll have to postpone my flight so Francesca and I can be in court."

"When will that be?" asked Rose.

He rubbed his forehead. "I have no idea."

"I don't understand why she is bothering us. It's over between the two of you, right?" asked Francesca. She never dreamt the women in Rudolfo's life would try and find him, but now one of them has. Not only finding him, but making her own daughter afraid to be outside her own home.

"Yes, Francesca, it's over." He took her hand. "I want only you."

"Then why is she doing this to Annie? I don't understand any of it," said Francesca.

Sensing they needed to be alone, Rose said, "I'll go check on Annie," and then walked to Annie's bedroom.

Rudolfo stoked the fire, then sat next to Francesca. "I don't understand any of it either." He looked at the fire. "I was so angry that I threatened her. I'm hoping that won't be held against me."

That was the confirmation that Francesca needed as she struggled with whether it was really over between Tina and him. If it wasn't over, he wouldn't have threatened her. "If they get Annie to comment in court, she can honestly say she's never seen you angry and neither have I."

"It's not a pretty sight, my love."

She laughed. "I still love you."

Rudolfo thought that even though they were engaged and planning their wedding, Francesca didn't know much about what he really did in Florence. So he changed the subject and decided it was as good a time as any since it was something he had wanted to talk to her about anyway since they had returned from New York. "As long as we're talking, you've probably wondered what I do for a living. I should tell you now in case I go to jail.

"I hope you don't," said Francesca. "You paint and have written books. Is there something else?"

"It's more than that, Francesca."

"Then tell me everything."

"I illustrate children's books, and merchants rent my prints to show in their studios. I'm in the middle of writing an instructional book on oil painting."

"I had no idea. I guess loving you was all that mattered to me. Will you be able to move to America with all you have going on?" asked Francesca, dreading the answer.

"I would just have to establish contacts here. Filipo is already managing the business part of what I do in Italy."

They talked more about his work, and then Francesca told him about her job and all that she did for the company. Feeling tired, she rested her head on Rudolfo's shoulder. The fire warmed them, and seemed to evaporate their troubles.

*   *   *

Francesca woke with a start after dreaming that someone had taken Annie. "Where's Annie?" she said.

Groggy, Rudolfo said, "She's safe."

"I want to see for myself." Both Francesca and Rudolfo went to her bedroom, but she wasn't there. Panic surged through them—where was she?

They went to the kitchen, and she wasn't there. "Oh, no, where is she, Rudolfo?" cried Francesca. They hurried to Francesca's bedroom, and no one was there. "What do we do now?" Tears were flowing down her face.

"Let's check the guest room." They saw Annie and Rose sleeping peacefully, unaware of the panic they had caused.

Francesca collapsed into Rudolfo's arms and started crying. "She's safe, my love," he said. There were tears in his eyes, and he felt like crying to release everything that had built up inside him. He couldn't bear to lose that little girl. He took Francesca's hand and led her to her bedroom. It had been a long night, and both were tired. Once they had laid down, sleep came quickly.

*   *   *

Francesca checked her work e-mails and saw that her boss wanted her to travel to Italy within the month. She smiled as she thought of traveling there with Rudolfo—but when would they be able to travel? Hopefully the court date would be soon and they could get on with their lives.

*   *   *

Two weeks later Francesca and Rudolfo were in court. Tina was sitting up front with her lawyer, and laughing about something he said, which only made Rudolfo angrier. He knew that he needed to calm down and not make a scene, then reminded himself that he was here for Annie, not for himself.

They stood as the judge entered the courtroom. The bailiff instructed everyone to be seated and then introduced the Honorable Michelle Jansen.

Francesca hoped that the judge had a daughter and would understand how it would feel if her own daughter was not safe.

Judge Jansen picked up a piece of paper. "Ms. Moretti, it has been brought to my attention that you are not a citizen of the United States. Is that true?"

"I can explain."

"Is that true or not?"

"Your honor . . ."

"Counselor, instruct your client to answer the question."

He whispered to Tina, and then she answered, "Yes, that's true."

"Do you work in the United States?"

"Yes."

"How did you get a job without being a citizen?"

"It's not really working; my boyfriend pays me in cash to help him at his studio."

The lawyer whispered to his client. "Why didn't you tell me about any of this?"

The sound of the gavel was heard throughout the room. "I'm the one in charge here—if you two want to argue, do it on your own time."

The judge continued. "Is your boyfriend a citizen?"

"I don't think so. He told me he had ways of getting around it."

Her lawyer grasped her arm and glared at her. "Don't say another word."

"You'd better listen to your lawyer. You are digging a deep hole for yourself and your boyfriend." said Judge Jansen. "Now let's talk about the charges that brought you here."

Before the judge could continue, Tina interrupted. "I didn't do anything."

"Counselor!"

"Do not say another word," Tina's lawyer cautioned her in a firm voice.

As Rudolfo observed the way Tina was acting, he was glad she had left him at the altar. My God, he thought, what a terrible mistake I could have made to marry her. He hadn't realized before that she had absolutely no common sense. Rudolfo sighed, took Francesca's hand, and held it tight.

"I will do the talking," warned Judge Jansen. "If you violate any of my requests I will have the bailiff lock you up."

The lawyer glared at his client.

"I see in the report that you stalked a little girl, twice, and parked outside her home on both occasions." The judge read more of the report. "Then you denied it at the police station after you were brought in for questioning. I would like to remind you, Ms. Moretti, that following a little girl around and parking in front of her house is stalking. I'm baffled as to why you would do such a thing. Can you enlighten me?"

"I was in Minnesota visiting my boyfriend's parents, who just moved here from Italy, and I went to the store and recognized Rudolfo. I thought we could get together and talk, but then I saw the girl. I was waiting for a good time to talk to him."

"So you stalked them both."

"No! I didn't stalk anyone. I just wanted to talk to him. I saw him in New York at Christmas and followed him around, and no one cared. Why is Minnesota so different?"

The judge shook her head. "There's nothing I can do about New York." She looked at Francesca. "Are you Annie's mother?"

Francesca stood. "Yes, your honor."

"How is your daughter doing?"

"She's better now that she knows the woman has been arrested."

"You can sit down," the judge said. She looked toward Tina and continued. "I will sentence you first on the fact that you are not a U.S. citizen, and are in this country illegally. Then I will sentence you for stalking a little girl." She looked at Tina's Attorney. "Any objections?"

"None, your honor." He just wanted to leave the courtroom and never see his client again.

"You will be deported back to Italy. Because you are working here and not paying taxes, your boyfriend will also be fined heavily and deported."

"What? You can't do that!" shouted Tina.

"Yes, I can do that."

Tina's lawyer put a firm grip on her arm. "Let the judge continue."

"Before you travel, you will be serving thirty days in jail here in Minnesota for the trauma you have caused the victim."

Tina stood up and started screaming at the judge. Her lawyer shook his head and put papers into his briefcase.

The gavel sounded, but that did not stop Tina from screaming. The judge said, "Bailiff, her sentence will be an additional thirty days; now take her away." The judge stood and immediately went to her chambers.

Her lawyer fumbled with the lock on his briefcase, and when he couldn't close it, he put the thick leather briefcase under his arm and practically ran out of the courtroom.

Rudolfo and Francesca remained seated and watched while an officer helped the bailiff handcuff Tina and escort her out. She glared at Rudolfo and screamed at him in Italian, and it was Rudolfo's turn to smile.

It was quiet now. Rudolfo and Francesca sat in silence for several minutes. Rudolfo was at peace now—he could leave and he knew Annie would be safe. He looked at Francesca. "Thank you for being you."

"I love you." She kissed his lips. "Let's go home so we can be with Annie. I know she's worried about what's happened in court."

Rudolfo smiled. "You have an amazing little girl, Francesca. I'm honored to be a part of your family." He looked into her eyes. "Once I get to Italy I'll make sure to get a restraining order against her there, too. I don't ever want to see her again."

Chapter Twenty-Three

Rudolfo worked for several days straight to get caught up on his illustrations. He was happy to be home, but what really made him happy was that Francesca had come with him. They made love every night, drank coffee and ate biscuits every morning with Filipo. Then Rudolfo would go back to his apartment to work and Francesca would go to shoe designers in the area, and order for the stores back home.

Rudolfo was looking at his illustrations and realized that the little girl he had drawn throughout the book looked just like Annie. He looked at his watch and decided to call her. With the time difference, she was about to go to bed.

He quickly went to the phone and dialed. "Hello," Annie said.

"Annie, I miss you."

"Grandma! Grandma! Rudy's on the phone! Rudy, when are you and Mom coming home?"

"I'm not sure. You, miss me, no?"

"I miss you, yes!"

Now that Rudolfo had heard her voice, he realized just how much he did miss her, and hearing that she missed him made him smile.

"Where's Mom?"

"She'll be back soon, she's working."

"Can I come to Italy?"

"Yes, after school is out in June."

"That's a long time, Rudy."

"I know, but it will be better when you don't have to make up so much homework."

"Okay," said Annie in a saddened voice.

"I called to say goodnight."

"I want to tell Mom something, but I'll tell you so you can tell her, okay?"

"Okay."

"I got an A when I told the class about our trip to New York. My teacher didn't believe we did all that until she called Grandma, and Grandma told her we did."

"I'm very proud of you, and I'll tell your mom. She'll be proud of you, too."

"I'll take the phone in my room. Tell her to call me when she gets home."

"You'll be sleeping. I'll have her call you in the morning before school."

"Okay, Dad. Love you. Arrivederci."

"Love you back. Arrivederci."

*   *   *

Tonight the three of them were going to a black-tie event in the gallery where Rudolfo's paintings were being displayed. Filipo and Rudolfo wore their black tuxedos, and Francesca wore a form-fitting long black dress. Her curly hair was down and flowing over her shoulders.

Francesca was in awe of Rudolfo's paintings. She had seen the ones in his cramped studio in his apartment, but had no idea of the extent of his talent. If there were people in the painting they looked lifelike, as if they were moving along the scene to capture the ambiance he was painting.

A man walked up to them, interrupting her thoughts,. "Ah, Rudolfo Vittori!" He bowed. "I hear you were traveling in the States. I'm happy to see you here."

"Yes, I was. I would like you to meet my fiancée, Francesca Jones. Francesca, this is Bernardo Russo."

Bernardo took Francesca's hand, then turned to Rudolfo. "This is your lovely lady displayed in the foyer. You have not done her justice." He kissed her hand and let it go. He focused again on her face. "It's so good to meet you." Then he was gone.

"Rudolfo, what's he talking about? What picture?"

He took her hand and led her to the foyer. The painting had not been displayed when they had come in earlier. He walked her to the middle of the entryway, and a painting of Francesca in an ornate gold frame filled the large wall.

Francesca was depicted standing with her thick curly hair blowing behind her, a white gown flowing from her shoulders. Her features were delicate but precise. The only colors in the picture were those of her blue eyes and red lips.

When Francesca could talk, she said, "You didn't . . . even know me, had never met me." She forced her eyes away from the painting and looked at him. "How could you . . ."

"How could I paint you? Oh, my love, it was easy. After I saw you on the bridge and watched you for a long time I went home and obsessed about you. You were in my thoughts day and night. When I couldn't sleep for several days I went to my studio and painted you." He gestured toward the painting, "And that's how I saw you in my mind. It's been locked up here at the studio. The one you saw at my apartment was something I painted afterward so I could see you anytime I wanted.

Francesca had no idea of the intensity of Rudolfo's feelings. She put her hand on his arm. "Do you think anyone will buy it?" On the other paintings, the price varied from fifty thousand, to one hundred thousand euros. She did not see a price on the painting before her.

He took her hand and looked at her intensely. "There will never be a price on the torment I felt not finding you and the joy I now feel loving you."

Taken aback by his sincerity, she could not look away from him until another of Rudolfo's followers called his name.

"Rudolfo, where have you been?" Their gaze broken, he turned toward the voice. "My wife called you several times to come to dinner."

"I've been traveling with my fiancée, Francesca." He turned to her. "Francesca, this is Julio Ferrari. He and his wife, Agnes, make sure I eat properly."

Julio took her hand and kissed it. "Your painting is stunning, but I'm afraid Rudolfo has not captured all your beauty. He will have to sell it to me and try again."

The two men laughed. A short, stout woman joined them, and Agnes was introduced to Francesca. "Ah," she said, "I thought there had to be a good reason why Rudolfo hadn't been over to eat. Most of the time he comes without an invitation."

"She is the best cook," Rudolfo said. He looked at Francesca. "Even better than Carmella, but don't you tell her that."

"Your secret is safe with me."

"Why don't you both come over tomorrow night? I've been needing a reason to make some of my garlic bread."

Julio was the first to respond, "You can make that anytime, Agnes. You don't need Rudolfo there."

Agnes laughed. "Will you come?"

Rudolfo looked at Francesca, "Yes, we'd love to."

When the arrangements were made, Rudolfo showed Francesca the rest of the gallery. People kept coming up to Rudolfo. Francesca had learned much about him during this trip, and she wondered if she could take him away from it all. Could she ask him to live in America now that she knew he had so many friends and followers? She would feel terrible, but she thought there might just be a way. She sorted it out in her mind during the evening.

*   *   *

"Agnes is a very good cook, and that garlic bread . . . words can't describe it," said Francesca. "You have nice friends. I hope they didn't mind us leaving early."

"She knows you have an early flight tomorrow," said Rudolfo.

When they got back to the apartment, Rudolfo made tea while Francesca sat at the table trying to organize her thoughts about a solution to their problem of where to move. He brought the cups of tea to the table.

"I had a great evening," she said. "How often do you have showings?"

"Not that often. Filipo usually arranges for me to go to galleries to try to sell them my work. He also arranges for radio and television interviews, but I haven't had one of those in a long time."

"I feel as if I've really gotten to know you this trip. I'm fascinated by what you do."

"That means a lot to me, Francesca." He poured more tea. "But you look troubled. What else is on your mind?"

She looked up at him, amazed that he could read her mind, but this was the opportunity she was waiting for, so she started. "I might have a solution to our moving."

He sat down. "I'm listening."

"We'll keep your apartment, and we can live here when Annie is out of school, and I'll see if I can work from here in the summer." She sipped her tea. "You can continue to have showings and interviews and keep in contact with your friends." She looked at his face and found acceptance, so she continued. "We possibly could move to New York. Mom and Jerry are serious about each other and Annie would be close to her cousins, and you can be close to Carmella."

Rudolfo thought about what she had said, then nodded, "I think that would work. Have you thought this through? I don't want you to have any regrets."

"I can think of plenty of reasons why I don't want to leave Minnesota, but none of them are valid when I think of loving you."

"What are your regrets?" He went to the cupboard for some honey, then came back and sat next to her. "We should talk about them, too."

"I'd have to clean and sell the house. I would have to make new friends in New York and here in Florence. What if Mom doesn't want to move to New York with us? What if Annie gets homesick and misses her friends?" She studied Rudolfo's face while he thought through what she had just said.

"After the wedding," he said, "Carmella would stay and help you clean, paint, whatever you want her to do." He smiled. "Even things you don't want her to do. Agnes and Julio have never had children and I know they will enjoy pampering Annie. Also, they know a lot of people, so I don't think you have to worry about making friends or being bored."

He went on, "Your mom might not move with us but I'm sure it won't be long before Jerry asks her to marry him, and with us already in New York she probably won't hesitate to say yes." He poured some more tea. "Let's make sure Annie gets back to Minnesota to see Grace. Then, too, we can have Grace come to New York for visits."

"Listening to you makes it seem so simple. I guess I'm just nervous. I've never had to make so many difficult decisions in my life."

"We have time before we decide what we are going to do," he said, smiling at her. "Your next decision should be an easy one. Make love to me, no?"

"Yes!"

Chapter Twenty-Four

Rose and Francesca sat back and toasted the fact that all the arrangements for the wedding were done. In two weeks, family from New York would be coming and staying at Francesca's house. Jerry would be staying with Rose, and Carmella felt that Rudolfo should be staying with Rose as well.

"Are you excited that Jerry is coming?" she asked her mother. "It's not as if you haven't seen him since Christmas."

"Yes, I'm excited. After your father died, I never thought I'd fall in love again, but I guess we just never know what might happen to us."

"Do you think he'll ask you to marry him?"

"He's mentioned that it would be nice if we got married, but he's never asked me."

"Have you thought about moving to New York if we move?" asked Francesca.

"I think about it every day. It would be an easy decision if you and Annie were already there. I'll miss it here, but I've told my friends, and they've all encouraged me to move. It would give them an opportunity to travel to New York and not pay an expensive hotel bill."

Francesca laughed. "I've been getting the same response. We just have to be prepared for a lot of visitors."

Hearing her mom talk and seeing that she was so willing to move, Francesca felt it would be one less thing for her to worry about. Mentally she crossed it off her list of concerns as she poured more wine into their glasses.

*   *   *

A week before the wedding, Rose and Francesca went to the airport to pick up Rudolfo. They told Annie she couldn't take time off, with school almost out for the summer. They got coffee and waited by the baggage claim area.

"Annie's been so excited about the wedding," said Francesca. "She's been writing Giovanni every week. He told her his mom is making him wear a tuxedo. Annie wrote him explaining, or I helped her explain the long dress she was going to wear."

They both laughed. "I wonder," said Rose, "if they'll change into their jeans as soon as the wedding is over."

"That would be okay by me," said Francesca. She looked at the clock on the wall. In ten more minutes the plane would land. The two women continued to sip their coffee and talk about the wedding. Soon the carousel was moving. The people standing around it were anxious to get their luggage and go home, but there was no sign of Rudolfo.

They threw their empty cups into the trash, and walked around to see if they could see Rudolfo. They waited another thirty minutes in case he had gone to the rest room, or had stopped along the way to the baggage area, but still there was no sign of him.

"Okay, I can't do this again," Francesca said. She took her mother's arm. "We're leaving," and she pulled her mother toward the door.

"There has to be a good explanation," said Rose.

"Yes, he doesn't want to marry me! Now let's go home."

They drove in silence, and even after they arrived home, Francesca had nothing to say. Her daughter had been so happy knowing that Rudolfo was coming. She didn't want her little girl to be disappointed.

"Francesca," said Rose in a gruff voice, "you need to find out what happened so we have something to tell Annie. She's not going to settle for 'he doesn't want to marry me.'"

Francesca was close to tears. She was exhausted from working every day, then coming home and working on wedding plans, and now the groom wasn't going to show up.

"Call his cell phone, or call Carmella," said Rose. "Maybe she knows where he is."

"No, Mom," said Francesca, close to tears. She laid her head on the table and closed her eyes. "What are we going to tell Annie? She'll be heartbroken." We had a good time in Italy, she thought, and she hadn't detected that he wasn't coming to the wedding. She played the time in Florence over and over in her mind and could find no plausible explanation for Rudolfo not showing up.

"Francesca."

I don't understand, why me? She thought about the last time he hadn't come and realized that maybe he was sick again.

"Francesca," called a gentle voice, the one she heard when making love—but she knew she was imagining it.

"Francesca, it's me." She felt a hand on her shoulder, opened her eyes and saw Rudolfo. She was up and in his arms kissing his face as tears flowed down her cheeks.

"Where were you? We waited a long time."

"I was delayed getting off the plane when one of the passengers tripped and hit his head. Then he sat back down next to me, blocking my way out. He was feeling dizzy and I didn't want him to stand up to move. I was so concerned for him that I didn't think to call. By the time he got medical help and left the plane, you had already gone. I called a cab."

He held her tighter. "I should've called you. I am so sorry, Francesca."

"I'm just glad you are here." She moved away from him. "Are you tired?"

"Yes, but I want to stay awake to see Annie."

"I'll go pick her up." Startled, Francesca looked at her mother, forgetting that she was still there. "I'll pick up something for dinner, too." Rose looked at Rudolfo. "It will be a while, so if you want to rest, go ahead, although I don't think I can distract Annie that long before she'll just want to come home and see you."

Rudolfo smiled. "I will stay awake until she gets here. We can always go out to eat later."

"I like your way of thinking," said Rose. "I have some errands of my own to run before I go to the school." She went to the door. "I'll see you later."

*　　*　　*

Annie talked a mile a minute when she came through the door and hugged Rudolfo. She told him about her day and said that there were three more days of school. Rudolfo knew of the countdown from their phone conversations.

"What will you do if you don't go to school? Your mother and I will have to put you to work, cut the grass, scrub the floors, wash the car, and whatever else we can think of."

"No, I think I'll play, go to Grace's house, and stay with Grandma."

Rudolfo laughed. "I'm tired from my trip. Will you wake me up in time to go eat?"

Annie said she would, and without thinking Rudolfo went down the hall to Francesca's room and crawled into bed.

"Hey, Mom," Annie said, "if you want to go to sleep, too, I'll wake you both."

It sounded like a wonderful idea. "Okay, I'll take you up on your offer." She gave Annie a high five and followed Rudolfo's path to her room.

*　　*　　*

Three days before the wedding, guests started arriving. Sylvia and Henry, Carmella and Tony's neighbors came. They were in Francesca's guest room. The children took over the downstairs to camp out where Rudolfo had usually slept and Carmella and Tony took Francesca's room.

Francesca, Jerry, Rudolfo, Filipo, and Julio and Agnes stayed with Rose. With four bedrooms, Rose had ample room for her guests.

The morning before the wedding, Francesca and Rudolfo were able to get away and have coffee. "I'm getting nervous," said Francesca. "We haven't decided yet on where to live. I guess that's not a problem, but if we decide to move we need to get Annie registered for school."

"What do you want to do?" asked Rudolfo.

"I guess that's why we haven't decided. I can't make up my mind."

"Do you really want to marry me?"

"Yes, I do."

"Then where we live doesn't matter."

She took his hand and held it to her chest. "I love you so much."

Rudolfo asked, "Are you ready for tonight?"

"I'm ready," Francesca answered. "I just hope the rehearsal and the dinner go well."

"I'm sure they will. Carmella doesn't know how to act since we've ordered the food from Totino's for the groom's dinner tonight. She was expecting to cook."

Francesca had a serious look on her face. "I hope you don't expect me to cook like she does, because you'll be very disappointed." Rudolfo laughed. "And I'm going to stay at my house tonight. It's bad luck for the groom to see the bride before the wedding."

"It's bad luck for me not to."

"You'll survive. We'll have a lifetime together."

"You're right. We'd better get back before my sister thinks we've eloped." Rudolfo looked out the window before he got up to go and laughed again. "Look, Francesca."

Annie and Grace were coming through the door with the De Luca children and Grace's brother, Jason, following behind them. "Hey, Uncle Rudy! Where have you been?" asked Franco.

"I'm hiding out before the wedding."

"That's funny," said Grace.

Annie got very close to Rudolfo and whispered in his ear. "Dad, I was telling everyone about the good scones, and everyone wants one, and I didn't bring enough money. Can I have some?"

He turned his head and whispered, "Sure, let's go outside."

Once outside, Rudolfo gave Annie more than enough money for everyone to order something. They went back into the store, and Francesca and he said their good-byes and left the children to themselves.

*　　*　　*

The wedding party practiced the procession several times. While the bride and groom were still at the altar, Father Tony Mitchell asked them if they were ready to get married. He also wanted to know how Annie was doing having a man in the family, but he noticed that the interaction with Rudolfo was favorable.

Father Mitchell turned to Francesca, saying, "The Vittori family will be good for both you and Annie."

He looked at Rudolfo. "And you are a lucky man. Be good to them both and your marriage will last a lifetime."

"I will," answered Rudolfo.

"Now kiss the bride. I'm sure the practice will do you good."

They kissed, and Father Mitchell interrupted. "Now let's go eat. I haven't eaten all day."

Everyone laughed and went down to the dining hall. Lasagna, spaghetti, salad, and garlic bread had been ordered from Totino's restaurant. Arlene, from the church, had volunteered to serve the food and make sure everything went smoothly. Rose had purchased several different desserts to be served after dinner.

The first thing on everyone's mind was eating. The older children pulled several tables together so they could all sit together. Rudolfo and Francesca went around to all the tables to visit.

"Filipo, why don't you get married?" asked Tony.

"No! No! I too busy for that nonsense."

"Nothing beats a good woman waiting for you when you get home," added Henry.

"Especially if she's a good cook, like my Carmella."

"And my Agnes is a good cook," said Julio.

"That's why I come to your house and not have to get married."

Rudolfo shook his head. "You're hopeless."

*　　*　　*

It was a late night, but even after people got home they stayed up and talked. Francesca went back to her house after several protests from Rudolfo.

In the morning, it was so noisy with all the children and adults that Francesca couldn't concentrate on her wedding day. She called her mother. "I need to go where it's quiet. Any ideas?"

"Come back here—most everyone went out for breakfast. I can sneak you in so Rudolfo won't even know you are here."

"Thank you! I'll be right there."

Chapter Twenty-Five

Holy Cross Church on University Avenue in Northeast Minneapolis was where the wedding was to take place. There were bows in peach and white tied to the ends of the pews. The hall downstairs was decorated in the same colors with balloons and rose petals on each table.

The groomsmen, the ring bearer, and the ushers, Antonio and Franco, wore black tuxedos with peach cummerbunds.

Francesca's strapless long white chiffon dress clung to her slim figure. The white embroidered roses accented the bodice and bottom of her gown with vertical sprays.

Her hair was pulled away from her face and clipped in the back with Francesca's grandmother's barrette. She wore her emerald necklace she got from Rudolfo, and Rose lent her daughter her diamond bracelet. She carried a bouquet of white and peach roses.

Amy, Grace's mom, and Carmella wore dresses in the same peach color, but different styles. Amy's was strapless, clung to her figure and hung just below her knees. Carmella's dress was full length with mid-length sleeves. Even though she had a trim figure, she felt that she shouldn't be showing anything off after having so many children.

Annie's dress was long, in the same peach color as those of the bridesmaids. Sylvia buttoned Annie's dress, tied the long sash in a bow in the back, and pinned on her peach and white carnation corsage. "You look lovely, little lady," Mrs. Ryan said.

"Thank you, Mrs. Ryan." Annie went over to her jeans, pulled something out of the pocket, and handed it to Sylvia. "Will you put this on for me, please?"

Sylvia smiled when she saw the yellow fire truck pin. "Sure, hold still." When it was on, she told Annie she could go into the church.

"Okay, thanks—bye." Annie took her basket with the rose petals and skipped out the dressing room door.

*   *   *

Giovanni was tugging at his collar. "Annie, can you make my bow tie looser? I feel like I'm choking."

Annie looked at it, untied the bow, and pulled on his collar. "Hey, there's a button." She undid the button. "Does that feel better?"

He nodded. She retied the tie in a lopsided bow. "You saved my life," he said. He pulled something out of his pocket. "Look Annie, your kaleidoscope. I carry it with me all the time." He handed it to her.

Annie held it up to the stained glass windows. "Wow!"

*   *   *

The photographer wanted to take pictures before the ceremony, but Francesca was so superstitious about Rudolfo seeing her, that she asked that the pictures be taken of the bride and her family, then the groom and his family. The pictures of the two groups together would be taken after the ceremony.

"Carmella, have you seen Rudolfo?"

"What do you mean, Filipo? Wasn't he with you getting ready?"

"No. I'm worried. I thought he was running late, but he not show up."

Carmella panicked. "What are we going to do? Did you call his cell phone?" Without waiting for an answer, she dug out her phone and dialed his number. Several rings later it went to voice mail. She tried it again, no answer.

"Does Francesca know he's not here?"

"I not think so. I not tell her."

"I'll see if they can take Francesca's family pictures first. Hopefully he'll show up by then. That brother of mine had better have a good explanation." She turned and stomped off toward the photographer.

*   *   *

He poured the man another drink. "Tell me again why you're not already at the wedding."

"Because the last time I was supposed to get married, the woman left me at the altar and I don't want to go through that humiliation again."

"Is it the same woman?"

"No. This woman is my lovely Signorina that I love with all my heart."

"Does she love you?"

"Yes, she does."

The bartender shook his head. He'd heard strange stories before, but he'd never had in his bar a groom who loved the bride, not showing up for a wedding. The guy's cell phone had rung a couple of times but he hadn't answered it. The bartender wished he knew who to call to come and get him. He drove up in a cab and the bartender thought that was strange, and now he'd decided that the whole situation was strange.

"Where's the rest room?"

"Down the hall. I'll save your drink for you."

When he was sure the guy had entered the rest room, he picked up the cell phone and selected the number from which the last call had been made.

"Hello, Rudolfo, where are you? You'd better have a good explanation."

"Miss, this isn't your friend, but he's here. He's got cold feet," said the bartender. He gave the address of the bar and hung up just before Rudolfo came back and sat down.

Ten minutes later Carmella and Filipo entered the bar and walked over to him. Carmella yelled at her brother in Italian.

"Save me, Filipo," Rudolfo said.

"You're on your own," Filipo answered. "Now let's go to the church before Francesca knows you're missing."

"She's probably not even there. I'll just stay here."

"On your feet, my friend. She is at the church and is as beautiful as ever. She's in love with you and can't stop talking about you. You already know what it's like to be left at the altar—don't do this to Francesca."

That comment stung Rudolfo's entire being. He remembered how he had felt and did not want the woman he loved to be left at the altar. Tears ran down his face as he got up and left the bar. Filipo took Rudolfo's arm and helped him into the car.

*   *   *

Carmella and Tony walked Rudolfo down the aisle. Once up front, Rudolfo stayed in the middle while Carmella and Tony stood on opposite sides. Filipo, the best man, and Amy, the maid of honor, were next. Arm in arm they joined the others.

The white runner was rolled down the aisle. Annie and Giovanni lined up and then started the long walk to the front. Annie dropped peach rose petals from her basket, and Giovanni fidgeted with the pillow on which the wedding rings were tied in place.

Rudolfo didn't see any of what was going on. He was distracted by his thoughts. Is Francesca going to show up? Will I be left at the altar again? That's probably why I couldn't see her before the wedding. It would be easier for her not to show up at all.

The alcohol was blurring his thoughts. There was no one else to walk down the aisle, and he didn't see Francesca.

Henry and Sylvia were sitting in front, and he didn't see Rose, either. Maybe she was at home trying to talk her daughter into coming to the church. After a few more painful minutes he was about to run off, when someone took his hand. He looked down. It was Annie, with a big smile on her face.

Francesca wouldn't leave both of us at the altar, he thought. He was feeling somewhat relieved. The organist started playing "Here Comes the Bride," and there she was in the back of the church with her mother. His tears were of joy, and flowed freely down his face.

∗   ∗   ∗

"Are you nervous, Francesca?" whispered Rose.

"Very. My hands are shaking, and my knees feel like I'll never make it to the front of the church."

"That means you are ready."

She glared at her mother. "Then I shouldn't be feeling so miserable."

Rose laughed. "You'll be fine. So, are you ready?"

"I'm ready."

Rudolfo couldn't take his eyes off her as she walked down the aisle. My lovely Signorina. He could feel the sweat running down his back and realized he had nothing to worry about. He rubbed his hands over his face and realized that this was real—his wife-to-be was coming to meet him, and soon they would be joined in matrimony.

He marveled at how lovely she looked: her white dress, her hair, her flowers. The sight of her took his breath away.

Once at the front, Rose gave her daughter a hug and a kiss on the cheek, and then sat down. Francesca waited for Rudolfo to come to her and take her hand, but he didn't move. He looked distraught and pale, and she thought that he would faint at any minute.

Filipo went to his side, held him up, and eased him over to a chair. Rudolfo put his head between his legs, and when the nausea passed and the cold sweats went away, he was able to stand. Filipo whispered in his ear that it was time to go to Francesca and bring her to the altar. Rudolfo nodded.

He went to her and held out his hand. She took it. Though he wanted to tell her how .sorry he was, he didn't think he could speak right now. But his eyes said it all. She kissed him on the lips and said, "I love you." He nodded.

Father Mitchell whispered to Rudolfo. "Should I begin?" Rudolfo nodded again.

"We are gathered here together in the sight of God . . ."

Rudolfo held tight to Francesca's hand. She was worried about him; he looked so pale.

Rudolfo couldn't shake the feeling of abandonment. Panic was rioting within him and he started to feel queasy again. Francesca was right next to him, and there was no threat of her leaving him alone. He decided he needed to shake this feeling so he didn't ruin their wedding day. He tried to calm his racing heart, and after several deep breaths, some of the color returned to his face.

Father Mitchell himself wondered if the groom would make it through the ceremony and decided to hurry it along.

"Rudolfo, do you take Francesca Ann Jones to be your lawfully wedded wife?"

He nodded, but he knew he had to say the words. Carmella was staring at him, and he knew he would be in trouble if he didn't speak. He forced the words, "I do." More than anything, he wanted her for his wife, and didn't know why his body was acting this way. "I do," he said again with more determination.

"Francesca, do you take Rudolfo Antonio Vittori for your lawfully wedded husband?"

"I do," she said without hesitation.

"I now pronounce you husband and wife." He lowered his voice. "If you feel up to it you may kiss the bride." The wedding party laughed.

Feeling much better, Rudolfo smiled and said, "I feel up to it."

She felt his lips touch hers like a whisper that grew more intense; then he released her and took her hand. They faced the congregation and walked back down the aisle. The wedding party followed. The bride and groom went back to the front and stopped at each pew so that their family and friends could congratulate them.

The reception was downstairs, but there were more pictures to be taken, so the wedding party left to meet the photographer at the Grain Belt Brewery on Broadway and Marshall, several blocks from the church.

All seven children were told to line up on the bridge overlooking the pond and flower garden. Giovanni and Annie stood next to each other in the middle and the rest lined up on either side.

* * *

"I'm so sorry, Francesca." Rudolfo, now out in the fresh air, didn't feel sick at all. "This was to be our special day, and I really messed it up. Will you ever forgive me?"

"No need to be sorry," said Francesca. "Kiss me and all is forgiven."

He smiled at her, then kissed her. "All is forgiven? Yes?"

"Yes, all is forgiven."

He saw Carmella approaching and he knew his sister wouldn't forgive him so easily. "Rudolfo, you scared me." She hugged him, then held him at arm's length. With tears in her eyes she said, "Congratulations, my brother. It appears you are just fine now. I'm so happy for you."

She turned to Francesca. "Do Annie and Grace know they will be coming to New York with Rose while you two are on your honeymoon?"

"No, but Amy knows. We were going to tell them at the reception. I was afraid Annie wouldn't be able to concentrate during the wedding if she knew."

*　　*　　*

The cake was cut, pictures were taken, and now everyone was seated and about to eat when someone clanked their fork on a wine glass. Rudolfo helped Francesca up, held her close, and gave her an intimate kiss. When the clapping started, they sat down.

Two hours had passed when the bride, groom, and Amy went over to the table where Annie and Grace were sitting. Rudolfo gave Annie and Grace a high five. "You ladies look very nice." He looked at Annie. "Your mother and I are leaving for our honeymoon now."

"Okay, Mom and Dad," Annie said, with a sad look on her face. "I'll miss you. How long are you going to be gone?"

"Two weeks," answered Francesca, then nodded to Amy.

"What do you girls think of going to New York with Grandma Rose and staying with Annie's cousins?" asked Amy.

They leapt out of their chairs and jumped up and down. Annie let out a squeal. Giovanni, who had overheard, joined them.

Annie went over to Rudolfo. "How long do we get to stay?" she asked him. She looked at Grace. "When do we get to go?"

"You'll go in two days, and you get to stay two weeks."

"Yay!"

"Will you still miss us?"

"Uh, yeah, I guess so, said Annie"

"We'll see you in two weeks—now give me a hug," said Francesca.

The bride and groom said their good-byes and left the reception, changed clothes at Rose's house, put their suitcases in the trunk, and started the four-hour drive north to Trail's End Resort.

Chapter Twenty–Six

The brilliant sun was setting, and in its wake left rich hues of red and white in the sky. A hint of freshly mowed grass filled the air. Sounds of boat motors could be heard while vacationers docked their boats before night fall.

The owner showed them to their cabin. It was large, with many windows on both sides. "The Anderson family built it, put in all the windows, and eventually sold it to us. There's a lot of room for two people, but it's the only cabin we have right now. You'll enjoy the deck out front overlooking the lake."

"The view is beautiful," said Rudolfo.

The cabin had a fireplace in the living room, a large kitchen, and a huge bedroom. There was another room with six twin beds and still had plenty of room left over for sleeping bags and suitcases. Windows were everywhere, so no matter where you were in the cabin you had a great view of the woods or the lake.

"Will you need a boat?"

"Yes," said Francesca without thinking. She remembered the great time that she and Annie had had last year when they rented a boat. They had fished and sometimes just anchored the boat and read while they took in the sun.

The owner looked at Rudolfo. "You'll be driving the boat, correct?"

"No, my wife is quite capable, and I'm sure no harm will come to your boat."

"Uh, okay." Shaking his head, he pointed to the dock. Luckily it was lit, so she could see the general area of the boat. "It's number two."

"Thank you. Is there a place to eat dinner? I know it's late."

"Just down the road is another resort with a restaurant that's open all hours. You can walk or take the boat over there. The boat has lights on it." He left to go, then turned back. "Enjoy your stay. Let us know if you need anything."

"Thank you. We will."

They watched him walk back to the main building. "Now tell me about your boating experience."

"I'll tell you at dinner," she said.

"Are we walking or boating over?" He asked. "Do I need a life jacket and my fishing pole?"

Francesca laughed. "Let's walk. We'll fish tomorrow."

*　　*　　*

The log cabin lodge was one big room, with a pool table, two ping-pong tables and video games on one side, and the restaurant on the other. There was a fireplace on one wall, and opposite was a large picture window overlooking Bowstring Lake. Rudolfo and Francesca ordered burgers and fries and sat in silence as they looked out at the lake.

Rudolfo was glad they had decided not to go on a big trip for their honeymoon. They'd talked about Hawaii and the Bahamas. They had even discussed a cruise to Mexico. It all seemed too hectic—planes, rental cars, ports of call.

It was Carmella who had suggested taking advantage of the Minnesota lakes and resorts. Francesca knew the perfect place, and so far it was.

Their concentration was broken when the waiter brought their food. "Now tell me, my love, how I came about marrying a woman who loves boats."

Francesca smiled at him. "I've always known how to drive a boat. My dad loved to fish, and being an only child, I was always along whenever he went fishing and I wasn't in school. I put my own worms on the line . . ."

"Yuck," interrupted Rudolfo, "those little squirmy things?"

She laughed, "Yes, those little squirmy things." They ate for a couple of minutes. "Then he taught me how to drive the boat so he could concentrate on fishing."

"I'll be glad to drive the boat while you fish. Are we going to eat them, too?"

"Of course, that's the best part. I'll teach you how to put the worms on the hook, and we can get some leeches or even . . ."

"Stop! I'm still eating. Like I said, I'll be happy to just drive the boat."

"Speaking of driving, you'll need to get a driver's license once we decide where to live."

"I get around by bicycle, cab or bus, in Florence. Maybe in New York City I could do the same, but not by Carmella's house, and it doesn't seem possible in Minnesota."

"Let's decide where we are going to live first and then we'll talk about you driving." She put catsup on her fry. "Okay, finish eating—then we'll talk about cleaning the fish." Rudolfo rolled his eyes.

When they finished eating they strolled back to their cabin. The stars were brilliant and lit their path. No more talk of fishing or boating. They both anticipated what was going to happen when they were alone. They hadn't unpacked yet, but there was plenty of time for that tomorrow.

They stopped in front of the cabin door. "I'll have to carry you over the threshold," said Rudolfo.

She smiled. "Okay, if you think you're up to it. I can always walk."

He swept her up in his arms, opened the door, and kicked the door closed behind them. His pace picked up as he walked the long hallway to the bedroom and laid her on the bed.

"It's hard to believe we are married, Francesca." He looked into her dark blue eyes. "So much heartache in my past, and when I feel such joy with you it's hard to believe it's really happening."

"So much heartache in both of our lives. We finally found our place of belonging, after all." She touched his face. "It is real, Rudolfo. We have to believe it and enjoy every minute of it."

"Let's start now, shall we?" He pulled her shirt over her head, unbuttoned her jeans, and continued until all her clothes were on the floor. He stood and took off his clothes and lay beside her. "I love you."

She turned and kissed him urgently, and when she stopped, it left his lips burning for more. His lips quickly connected again with hers and they continued kissing, but it didn't relieve the burning sensation that now moved through his whole body. He touched her breast and fondled her nipple, then his hand moved down to her stomach. He gently moved on top of her. She let out a groan. Rudolfo's tongue made a path from her neck to her stomach.

"Rudolfo!"

That's all he needed to hear, and he was on top of her again. "Ah, my love."

She held tight to him as he kissed her and made love to her.

Love flowed through her like warm honey. Fulfillment inched through their veins.

*   *   *

Their bodies were still moist from their lovemaking. When they stopped, it was early morning, and they were now fast asleep. Mid-afternoon, Francesca awoke and noticed that Rudolfo wasn't beside her. She rubbed her eyes and looked at the antique clock next to the bed. She couldn't believe it was almost four o'clock. She put on her robe and sandals and found him painting. His canvas was propped up on the easel in front of the large picture window in the living room. The scene was of the lake.

He had only briefs on. The body that made her own flesh hot when he touched her was in full view. Her pulse quickened. She considered pulling him back to bed with her, but she didn't want to break his concentration.

She'd never seen such passion and talent in anyone, and he could paint anything, even a fire truck. His strokes were light, and he seemed to paint without thinking—but she knew by the tenseness of his forehead that he was concentrating fully on what he was doing.

She went to the kitchen and noticed that coffee was already made. She poured herself a cup and went outside and sat on the bench swing. She held the cup between her hands on her lap and took several deep breaths of the fresh warm air.

The lake was still, mirroring trees and cabins along the shore. The ripples from the fishing boat across the lake interrupted the calmness and left the mirrored images swaying back and forth in its wake.

Her eyes went to the dock with the boats. It was time to take Rudolfo for a ride. She was hungry and craved another meal like the burgers and fries they had the night before. This time they would take the boat. Tomorrow they would go fishing. She smiled just thinking about it.

It was so good to get away from the city, she thought, but she missed Annie. She decided to call her. Then they would eat.

Once inside, Francesca noticed Rudolfo was no longer in front of the window. She went over to the canvas. He had captured exactly what she had seen on the lake moments earlier, even the boat. Standing in front of the easel, she could smell his earthiness, then felt his touch on her shoulder. She turned around.

"Good afternoon, my love."

"You kiss me, no?" asked Francesca.

"I kiss you, yes." And he did.

"Let's go to the resort and eat. I'm famished."

"Do I have to put on a shirt?" he asked.

"No, if I don't have to put on any clothes."

"Okay, I'll get dressed. I don't want anyone to see how lovely you are under that robe." He looked toward the bedroom. "The last one dressed has to pay."

She raced him down the hall and put on her clothes as fast as she could. Rudolfo was sitting on the bed watching her. "Hey, you're letting me win," she said.

He smiled at her and started dressing. "The enjoyment of watching you get dressed was more pleasure than having you pay for dinner." He took her hand and led her down the hall. "By the way, your shirt is on backwards." He let out a loud laugh and ran outside.

She came out with her shirt on the right way. "Just for that, we're taking the boat." She took his hand and led him to the dock. "Get in."

"Ah, we can walk."

"Get in."

Rudolfo got in reluctantly and sat down. Francesca sat by the motor and made sure there were two life jackets. She squeezed the primer bulb several times to get the gas into the motor, then pulled the starter rope until the motor took hold and started.

She unlatched the hooks attached to the ropes that were holding the boat to the dock, then pushed the boat away. She took the steering handle and eased the boat away from the other boats, then headed toward the resort. When she could finally relax a bit, she looked at Rudolfo. He was pale. His knuckles were white as he grasped the sides of the boat.

"Are you okay?" she asked, concerned.

"I'll be fine as soon as you land this thing."

She thought that if he was afraid of being in the boat, fishing was definitely out. "We're almost there. Hang on."

She tied up the boat at the restaurant dock and helped Rudolfo out. He pulled her into his arms and started laughing. "Fooled you!"

She pushed herself away and hit him on shoulder. "Brat!"

He threw back his head and let out a peal of laughter.

"You're not making any marriage points, my dear, by laughing at your bride."

He put his arm around her shoulders. "You still love me, no?"

"I still love you, yes."

They went in and sat down at the same table as the night before. "I forgot to call Annie," said Francesca.

"I have my cell phone. Why don't you call her after we order?"

Chapter Twenty-Seven

Carmella was making supper as the children were packing for their trip the next day. She was thinking about her brother. He's happy, she told herself. It's about time. I don't have to worry about him anymore, and even better is the fact he's moving to New York. At least that's what they said the last time I talked to them. The location seemed to change every time Rudolfo and Francesca had the discussion about where they would live.

Carmella knew Rose was ready to move to New York, but not until she was sure that her daughter and granddaughter were moving, too. Carmella hoped that when her children were grown they would all stay in New York. But it was too soon to think about that now. Startled when the phone rang, Carmella answered and called Annie to the phone.

*   *   *

"Hi Mom, when are you coming home?"

"Not for a while yet. What are you doing?"

"I'm packing. Mrs. Ryan is helping me. Grace is here, too. She's staying overnight so we can just go to the airport tomorrow. Mrs. Ryan is checking her suitcase, too, to make sure Grace has everything before we take off. What are you doing, Mom?"

"We took the fishing boat to the resort and are about to eat dinner. Tomorrow we might go fishing." She looked at Rudolfo. "Your dad loves to fish and touch the worms and leeches." She couldn't keep a straight face. "I really don't know if he likes those things, but we'll find out tomorrow."

"Tell Dad I want to talk to him."

"Hi, Annie."

"I'm going to tell you a secret about fishing. Ask the owner, I think his name is Greg, to give you some fishing gloves. That way you don't have to touch the worms or the fish when you take them off the hook. I use them all the time."

"That's good to know. I miss you, little one."

"I miss you, Dad."

"I'll let you talk to your mom again. I love you."

"Annie, be good. We'll come and pick you up in New York in about two weeks. Okay?" said Francesca.

"I'll be good. Have fun! See you later. Love you."

*   *   *

Francesca and Rudolfo made a campfire every night, roasted marshmallows, and made s'mores, but one night they ran out of graham crackers and chocolate. "We'll have to go into town and buy groceries. Then we can get bait. We really need to go fishing."

"I'm willing to give it a try," Rudolfo answered. "Just don't expect too much of me. Teach me how to drive the boat and you can fish to your heart's content." He turned serious. "Francesca, we need to decide where we are going to live. Annie needs to know where she's going to school next year."

"I know. It's hard to decide. Annie wants to go to New York, but she'll miss Grace. Mom wants to move to New York to be with Jerry, and if we're there it will make her decision easier. Carmella mentioned that she would be happy to have you close so she can keep an eye on you."

"But, where do you want to live? I don't want you to think about anyone else when you make your decision. You already know I'm fine with moving to New York and keeping my apartment in Italy for when we travel back and forth. You know, too, that I will stay in Minnesota if you ask me to. But what I don't know is where you want to live."

"I want to stay in Minnesota. They don't have lakes in New York, do they? I love coming up north and taking in the fresh air and being by a lake, going fishing, boating, or camping."

He smiled. "I never would've guessed that when I met you."

"Are you disappointed?"

"I could never be disappointed in you."

"We've decided to live in Italy during the summer when Annie is out of school. What I don't know is how to make everyone happy. Mom and Jerry are very serious, and it would be easy for her to move if we move. Annie is counting on the move." She took his hand. "That's why I can't make a decision."

"Ever since we arrived at the resort, I've been thinking," Rudolfo said. "I talked to Greg about real estate when you were taking a nap yesterday. He gave me a newspaper that lists all the cabins and land for sale in the area. I looked at each one of the listings. I wrote down an average price and then thought it might be nice to have a cabin by an airport, if there is an airport up here. We could just fly in and not have to worry about driving for hours to the cabin."

Francesca took a few minutes to think about what Rudolfo just said. If they kept his apartment in Italy, bought a house in New York, and bought a cabin in Minnesota . . . She knew she couldn't afford all this, but Rudolfo was getting thousands of dollars for just one painting. It would be so nice to come back to Minnesota. "Where will we get all the money?" she asked.

"I'll just have to paint more and tell Filipo to sell more." He smiled at her. "I've always wanted to buy a home of my own someday. I love being at the cabin, too. I'm glad you decided to come here on our honeymoon. If money were no object, would you consider my new plan?"

"Yes, I'll consider it." She looked at him. "Okay, I say yes, let's do it."

"We'll have to look at a lot of cabins this summer to decide which one would be right for us."

"We'll have to bring Annie with us."

"I sure do miss her. I wonder how she's doing. Should we call her?"

*　　*　　*

The next morning they got up early and took the two-hour trip to Brainerd. They found the airport off Highway 210, and after asking questions found out that they could fly into Brainerd from Minneapolis, then take a taxi to their cabin. Or there were storage garages where people keep a car so they can fly here and then drive to their cabin, then drive back and catch a plane back home.

A man at the airport gave them a map of the lakes in the area. Over lunch at a nearby restaurant, they studied the map and crossed out the lakes that were too big.

They found that the small town of Aitkin had more small lakes than the Brainerd area, so they headed to Aitkin. Once they arrived, they stopped in town to get listings of cabins for sale. The man working there offered to show them land and cabins.

Francesca was thankful for the realtors offer to drive; she needed a break. The cabins they looked at weren't in very good condition, so they decided to look at land and have a cabin built the way they liked. Francesca thought the first site they saw was perfect. The owners had been planning to build, but the wife had passed away and the man didn't want to go out there without her. Before she had gotten sick they had cleared the land, dug the well, and put in electricity.

They went back to town, decided to purchase the land, and signed the papers. They didn't have a down payment so they were instructed to go to the bank down the road and take out a loan. This took longer than they had expected because all of Rudolfo's references were in Italy. The banker was also having trouble with Rudolfo's accent, and Francesca had to interpret.

The banker gave them names of several contractors in the area to help them build their cabin. They returned to the real estate agency with the check, signed several more documents, and were given a packet of papers to keep. Then they were on their way back to Bowstring Lake.

After an hour on the road, Francesca broke the silence. "What did we just do?"

"I don't know. It all happened so fast. I'm glad you wrote down the directions to and from town, because I don't think I would be able to find it again."

"It's going to be a busy summer. I might have to quit my job," laughed Francesca.

"I would love for you to quit your job and be with Annie everyday, but only if you want to."

"I'll consider that, but first we have to think about getting something built. We'd have to have six bedrooms and three bathrooms for all the relatives."

"No, no! Two bedrooms, one bathroom. No one will know about the cabin but Annie and us. No visitors allowed."

"Your sister would hurt you if she ever found out."

He laughed out loud, "You're right."

They checked into a hotel in Brainerd and spent the night, exhausted with all the driving and the day's events. As they ate supper they talked about their plans and realized that now, more than ever, important decisions had to be made, not only about building but on where they would call home.

Chapter Twenty-Eight

Annie and Grace had fun the entire two weeks and didn't want to go back home. They even liked the chores, which meant that they could always be together. They folded towels, set the table, dusted, and kept Giovanni and Maria company when they went to the fire house to see Captain Ellis.

The day before they were scheduled to go back to Minnesota, they helped the Ryans clean their house. In return, Mrs. Ryan promised to take them to the store and buy them some candy. Annie and Grace made sure they did a good job, and Mrs. Ryan bought them not only candy, but also ice cream.

Rose, Jerry, Carmella, Tony, Rudolfo, and Francesca were sitting around Carmella's kitchen table. "You went to a cabin for your honeymoon, took a two-hour drive, purchased land, took out a loan, and went back and finished your honeymoon at Bowstring Lake?" asked Carmella.

"When you put it that way, it does seem a little strange," Francesca said.

"When are we going to be invited to this place?" asked Tony.

"We are only going to have a small cabin, two bedrooms and one bathroom. So you probably won't be invited." Rudolfo looked at Francesca. "It will be a place for the two of us to go, a private getaway."

"Well, isn't that nice," said Carmella. "Italian families are supposed to be close. That doesn't sound like you want to be too close."

Rudolfo laughed. "Francesca was right. She said you'd be upset." He smiled at his sister. "We already talked to the contractor and it will be big enough for you to visit."

As Carmella left the table to get more coffee, she hit her brother on the shoulder. "Don't mess with me, Rudolfo."

"That will be nice for all of us to get away," said Rose. "There's nothing like a family affair."

"Great . . ." said Rudolfo.

Their coffee cups were filled and Carmella sat back down. "When you come to America you really make a presence. Now where in New York are you going to live?"

Both Rudolfo and Francesca shrugged their shoulders. "I guess with you, Sis."

"You can live here, but you can't just sit around all day."

"I'm glad I have a job," said Tony. He looked at Rudolfo. "You'll have to find a job just so you can leave the house every day."

Chapter Twenty-Nine

Six Months Later

Francesca and Rudolfo decided to design the layout of the cabin themselves. In the fall Rudolfo stayed at a hotel to assist the builders.

The log cabin had a porch along the entire front of the cabin and now Christmas lights were embedded in the snow the length of the railing. The spacious living room with it's over sized couches and chairs had an impressive view of the bay. Today the sun was shining through the large picture windows, warming the room.

The cabin was modest looking; however, most of it extended into the woods and it was much larger than it appeared. There were six bedrooms with two double beds in each room. The master bedroom had a queen sized bed and was separate from the other bedrooms.

The kitchen was spacious with white cupboards, black and white marble counter tops and a walk in pantry. The stove had eight burners with a large capacity oven.

Three windows above the sink looked out at the woods and gravel road in the distance. The marble topped table, was large enough for ten people, with black wooden chairs and three hanging rod iron lights above it. Carmella had had a hand in designing the kitchen to fit her needs under the condition she would make Christmas dinner. She readily agreed.

The dining room table seated sixteen, and was on the opposite end of the living room by the kitchen. Plenty of room for the thirteen people seated for Christmas dinner.

When everyone was seated, Tony said grace before they ate their Christmas meal. The large table was in front of a spacious window overlooking the frozen Minnesota lake. Francesca got up to get a glass of water from the kitchen after the food had been passed around. "Where are you going?" asked Rudolfo.

"To the kitchen for some water, and I'm quite capable of getting it myself," she said.

"No, no, I'll get it for you," Rudolfo said. He went into the kitchen and returned with a glass of ice water.

"I didn't do everything for Carmella when she was pregnant, and all of our children turned out fine," said Tony.

"Actually, Tony did nothing."

"But Francesca is different."

"I'm not different," said Francesca to Rudolfo. "I'll be fine—now come over here and sit down. The baby is moving."

A big smile lit up Rudolfo's face. He put his hand on her stomach and felt the baby kicking. "Must be a boy, he feels so strong."

"Do you have any names picked out?" asked Rose. She had asked them last week, but they still hadn't decided on names.

"Not yet," said Francesca. "Since we don't know what the baby will be, we have to decide on a boy's and a girl's name."

"Me and Giovanni have two names you can use," said Annie.

"Yeah, we decided on Italian names. Annie, you tell what they are."

"For a boy, Bob. For a girl, Susie."

Giovanni and Annie laughed. "We think you need easy names," said Annie.

Rudolfo watched the two laughing, and it warmed his heart. Now a new baby would be born, something he'd wanted for a long time, even before he knew Francesca. He was thrilled that so many people would be able to share the joy with them.

"What do you think about the names, Francesca?" asked Rudolfo.

"They are lovely names, but they're not Italian. We could break tradition and have Norwegian names, like Ole or Sven."

That made everyone laugh. "We have four more months to decide. We should have something figured out by then."

The conversation continued, and everyone was offering names for the new baby. The children cleared the table and headed into the kitchen to do the dishes and clean up.

When it was dark, Rudolfo, Tony, and Jerry went outside and built a campfire while everyone sat in the living room in front of the window. It was below zero, and no one dared venture outside to sit around the fire. The younger children went down to the playroom to play with their presents while the older ones joined the adults.

*   *   *

"It's been a good day, Francesca," Rudolfo said. He held her close, but was careful. "I love you so much, Francesca. I wish the baby were already here. Maybe then you wouldn't be so tired."

"I don't mind being tired—I'm just glad the morning sickness is gone."

"Me, too. Annie and I were so worried about you."

"When I was pregnant with Annie I was alone and had no one to share the joy with when the baby moved, or get support from when I wasn't feeling good. Mom was a big help, but it's different this time. Our baby is lucky to have you for a dad."

If such love really existed between two people, he hadn't been aware of it until now. Every morning when he awoke he was happy to see his wife next to him.

Rudolfo had called Filipo and told him to find a signorina to marry. Filipo just laughed, saying, "Maybe I hang out on the Ponte Vecchio Bridge and find someone like you did." He laughed again. "You were so miserable every day when not finding your lovely lady. Was it worth it?"

"Yes, my friend, it was worth every moment of misery."

Now he was holding that woman, the one he had loved even before he met her and now loved more than life itself. And loved the new baby, growing and thriving inside the woman he loved. He didn't have a preference for a boy or girl, only for Francesca to stay well and for them to raise their new creation together.

"We're both lucky, Signorina. Ti amo, I love you."

She kissed him. "I love you too." She looked at him. "When you say you love Annie, you say 'ti voglio bene.' When you say you love me, it's 'ti amo.'"

"'Ti voglio bene' means I wish you well, as in family. 'Ti amo' means I love you with all my being."

"Ti amo, Rudolfo."

*   *   *

"I have an announcement to make," said Rose the next morning, above the talking at the breakfast table.

Jerry took her hand. "We have an announcement to make."

"Jerry asked me to marry him."

Maria jumped up and went over to her. "Grandma Rose, did you say yes?"

Rose smiled, "I said yes."

"Can I see the ring?"

"Ah," said Jerry, "I forgot it at home."

Maria took off the silver ring she had gotten for her birthday the month before and put it on Rose's little finger. "Here, Grandma, you can use this one until you get back home."

Rose hugged Maria. "Thank you, honey. I'll be sure to give it back when I get mine."

Carmella, sitting next to Rose, gave her a hug. "Congratulations." She looked at Jerry. "What took you so long?"

"Men don't hurry into such important matters. We have to make sure it's the right thing to do," said Tony.

"Then why did you ask me to marry you after two months?"

He laughed, "I was afraid you'd hurt me."

"I've been waiting for a year," said Rose.

"I wanted to make sure you'd say yes. If I took my time I thought you'd be begging me to marry you."

Rose laughed. "I almost did."

From across the table, Annie asked Jerry, "Will you be my grandpa now?"

"Will you be our grandpa, too?" asked Antonio.

"Of course I will," said Jerry with a shaky voice. With Annie he felt blessed to have another grandchild, and now he would have six more. Also he would have a beautiful woman to share the rest of his life. He had to admit that there wasn't much alone time with such a big family, but he enjoyed every minute with all of them. The alone times were that much more special.

"Now I'll have a father-in-law," said Rudolfo. "We can hang out and go bowling together."

Jerry laughed. "I think I'll pass on the bowling."

Chapter Thirty-One

Ten Years Later

The cement garage, empty of four fire trucks, was now filled with tables and chairs. Each table had a white tablecloth, balloons, confetti, and scattered bits of wrapped chocolate.

Captain Ellis was retiring from the fire department, and today was the day to celebrate. Carmella was doing the cooking, and this was proving to be quite an event.

"Giovanni, I have all the tables decorated. How are you doing with the streamers?"

"I have a few more to hang up." He stopped what he was doing and looked at Annie. "Do you still love me?"

"Yes, I do."

"Remember, you promised to marry me," he said.

"I remember, but we are going to college first."

"No, we should get married before that. I don't want to lose you to some college jock."

"I've known you since I was five. You won't lose me," Annie said.

He winked at her. "Good."

"Annie, when's Mom bringing little Rudy?"

Annie went over to her ten-year-old-sister. "In half an hour, Carina."

"When he gets here, tell him to come outside and help the firemen with the grilling."

"Are you sure they want you out there?" asked Annie, knowing that they had asked her sister and her eight-year-old brother to help.

"Captain Ellis already asked us."

"Okay, Carina Rose," said Giovanni.

"My name is Carina, and I'm going outside, so tell Rudy where I am." She stomped off, but had a smile on her face.

*　　*　　*

Francesca and Rudolfo were heading out the door. Rudy had already started walking to the station with Franco.

The last ten years of marriage had been good ones. They had two children—Carina Rose, who was named after Rudolfo's mother and Francesca's mother. Rudy was named after his father.

Henry and Sylvia decided it was time to move closer to their children in New Jersey, and sold their house to Rudolfo and Francesca, while Francesca was still pregnant with Carina. Annie was excited she would live so close to her cousins and could go to school with them. It was an easy decision for Rose to make to move with them.

Rose and Jerry did a lot of traveling with their grandchildren in the large camper they had purchased after they were married. There were times though, when they packed up the camper and left without telling anyone they were going until the next day.

Since Francesca was no longer working, she was able to be with Rudolfo when he traveled for his art shows and to visit his beloved

Florence, and keep in touch with Filipo.

*   *   *

"Wait a minute, Rudolfo," Francesca said. As he turned and faced his wife, she said, "I need to tell you something."

"Okay," he said, a little worried.

She took his hand. "I want to tell you that I love being your wife and having your children, and that I love you. Before I met you I felt like I just existed and had no meaning in my life, except for Annie. I feel now like I really belong."

"Ti amo, my love," said Rudolfo. He touched her face. "I feel that this is truly the place for us, together, after all."